W9-CXT-570

The sisters of the community marched in from the opposite door, their shoes tapping out a sure rhythm on the floor. The sound so pleased Abel that he looked down to watch their feet. As the last few entered, he saw with a shock that one of the girls was unshod.

Fascinated, he watched her feet move lightly under the blue of her skirt. Fearfully he let his eyes wander up the dress to her hands. They, at least were folded in proper Shaker style. . . . He looked higher, skipping quickly over the crossed white handkerchief on her breasts, past her neck to the heart-shaped face capped in white. . . .

She looked frightened, yet somehow defiant. He knew her name. Sara. He had seen her before, though he had never really noticed her. She was part of the family; that was all that had ever been important to know. But why was she barefoot? Had anyone else noticed?

"Yolen effectively individualizes her characters and evokes a vivid image, rich in fact-based detail, of a tightly structured Shaker haven. . . . powerful and provocative."

—*ALA Booklist*

Also available from VAGABOND BOOKS

The Gift of Sarah Barker

by
Jane Yolen

Vagabond Books

SCHOLASTIC BOOK SERVICES
New York Toronto London Auckland Sydney Tokyo

No part of this publication may be reproduced in whole or
in part, or stored in a retrieval system, or transmitted in any
form or by any means, electronic, mechanical, photocopying,
recording, or otherwise, without written permission of the
publisher. For information regarding permission, write to
The Viking Press, 625 Madison Avenue, New York, NY
10022.

ISBN 0–590–32418–7

Copyright © 1981 by Jane Yolen. All rights reserved. This
edition published by Scholastic Book Services, a division of
Scholastic Inc., 730 Broadway, New York, NY 10003, by
arrangement with The Viking Press.

12 11 10 9 8 7 6 5 4 3 2 1   2   3 4 5 6 7/8

Printed in the U.S.A.   06

For Marilyn,
whose gifts are
patience, loyalty, and love

❧ A Historical Note

In 1774 Ann Lee, an English mystic, came to America with a small group of followers who believed that she was the female incarnation of God, the "Bride of Christ." Her husband, Abraham Stanley, traveled with them but left the group soon after their arrival.

Ann Lee and her followers built a small community in the wilderness of northern New York. They called themselves the United Society of Believers in the First and Second Appearing of Christ, but other people called them Shakers because of their strange ecstatic religious meetings in which they sang, wept, shrieked, danced, shouted, and shook in their worship. So they took that name for themselves: Shakers.

That one Shaker community grew into many all across the face of the American countryside until, by 1850, there were six thousand members in nineteen separate places. From Maine to Kentucky, Shakers built their communal farms and lived and worked together. But the number of Shakers could not grow in any natural way because, along with their belief in Mother Ann's godhead, was their absolute conviction that men and women had to live rigidly separated lives. There could be no marriage, no sexual love, no babies. If a married couple wanted to join the Believers, they would henceforth live as brother and sister, giving all they owned to the community. Their own children would become their brothers and sisters as well. And though the head of the men was known as Father and the leader of the women as Mother, these were titles of respect and had nothing to do with procreation. Only by adopting children and adults into the Society could the Shaker numbers grow.

Yet grow they did, until the 1860s, when fewer and fewer folk joined them or dropped orphan children at their doors. By the middle of the twentieth century there were fewer than a dozen Shakers left alive.

But the legacy they have left America still lives: their joy in hard work, their inventions and handcrafts, their tuneful songs, their willingness to live a simple life.

The story of Sarah Barker and Abel Church is not a true story; there was no *real* Sarah Barker, no *real* Abel Church. But there were boys and girls like Abel and Sarah in every Shaker community. However, as loved as those children were by their brothers and sisters in the Shaker faith, only one or two in ten chose to remain Shakers all their lives. The rest left the Shaker communities when they reached adulthood to live in what the Believers called, witheringly, the World.

Just as Sarah and Abel are each a synthesis of many real Shakers, so New Vale is a mixture of many real Shaker farms. There is a fine, round stone barn still standing proudly at Hancock Shaker Village in Massachusetts and a Meeting House at Sabbathday Lake in Maine that looks very much like New Vale's own. And the ceremonies, rites, songs, and spiritual gifts described in this story are all based on real ceremonies and meetings as recorded by Shaker scholars, historians, and in the diaries of the Shakers themselves.

I have not used the plain language — the "thees" and "thous" — which most Shakers affected. And I have deliberately scanted on the long novitiate process that a would-be Shaker would go through, joining first a "gathering family," then a junior order, before becoming a full-fledged covenantal member of the Believers. The complex government of the Shakers is also just sketched here, as it is really only of minor interest to the story of Sarah and Abel.

Of course Sarah and Abel did not really live. But I like to think that if you walk through Sabbathday Lake on a spring afternoon, you might hear the sound of Sister Sarah's bare feet tiptoeing through the silent Dwelling House hall. Or that the happy note of her laughter blending with Abel's might come drifting to you on a south wind from the second story of Hancock's round stone barn some moonlit night in the spring.

April 27, 1854

New Vale, Massachusetts

❧ 1. Sarah

Sister Sarah Barker found the beginnings of spring on the edge of the half-acre clearing high up on Holy Hill. Low bush blueberries were starting to leaf out, and the rocky ground seemed peppered with patches of lichen green. She secretly reveled in that promise of buds and leaves and fruit. It satisfied her in a way that the full burst of coltsfoot and parsley, the early herbs in the carefully cultivated garden, did not.

A small brown bird with a smudge on its breast — an unshakerly smudge, she thought — hopped around inside the fence that guarded the Fountain Stone. Sarah tracked it patiently, cautiously, squatting back on her heels to regard it with silent pleasure, but she was careful never to set foot inside the hexagonal plot around the marble marker.

1

The bird looked back at her, unafraid, and came right up to her feet. She wriggled her toes at it, and it seemed to regard them as inedible but fascinating. Then it picked up its own spindly little feet one after the other.

Sarah could have reached out and touched the bird. Instead she whispered, "One foot up, the other down, tread the serpent to the ground." It was one of her favorite hymns.

The bird put its head to one side as if considering her whispered song as a statement. Then the silliness of it all overwhelmed Sarah, and she laughed out loud. The bird flew off into the bushes, where it scolded her with an insistent peeping.

Sarah put her hands up over her mouth, stood up, and looked around her secret kingdom one last time before starting down the hill. Every now and then she paused a little, as if remembering the way. But she had not forgotten it, even though the Believers mounted that particular hill only twice a year, May and September. The path was clearly marked by the hundreds of feet that had marched up and down it for almost thirteen years, spring and fall, in that holiest of processionals. Sarah's glance was more than a remembering. It was a holding look and a secretive look as well. She knew she must not be seen returning from a private trip up this forbidden hill.

Secrets were not the Shaker way. A secret trip was not a Shaker trip. Confession and obedience were the only conditions of forgiveness and salvation. How often had she been told that! Yet to Sister Sarah Barker, at fourteen, secrets had become the most important part of her world, the only part that belonged truly to her. And to God, she added hastily under her breath.

Sarah had thought a lot about her secrets lately. At night, conscious of the breathing of the other three girls near her, she had tried to promise herself to give away her secrets. Or to confess them to an eldress. Or speak them out or shout them out or sing them out in Meeting. But she had broken each promise to herself because to tell would be like taking a sharp knife and cutting off a limb or gouging out an eye. That sort of martyrdom would never be asked of her. Still, the community *did* ask for all her most private thoughts, and somehow, to Sarah, that seemed a worse mutilation.

She had been told over and over, first in the children's order and now as a member of the Church family, that secrets were wrong. "An open heart is a Shaker heart," Mother Jean was fond of saying. Secrets were as wrong as Sarah's persisting in adding the *h* to the end of her name. Not Sara but Sarah. It looked — prettier that way, she had thought when she practiced it in her careful handwriting. But useless. That extra *h* was unshakerly, adding nothing but beauty to her name.

She was thinking so hard about her secrets that she failed to notice a slight ridge in the path, a gnarled root that snaked alongside the rocks and had resisted the pressure of Shaker feet for years. She stubbed her toe on it, tripped, and plunged forward, falling heavily onto her knees and hands. Her heavy skirts protected her knees, but her palms scraped against the pebbles. Pain made her cry out, though she was not usually a weeper. When she stood up again and

3

looked at her hands, bleeding slightly and ingrained with dirt, the whimper turned into a moan. How could she explain *this* away? She would be caught again, just as she had been the first time. She had been about six years old then, sneaking down from Holy Hill. It had been a brilliant summer's morning, and her mouth was smeared with berries.

"Sister Sara, where have you been?" It was Sister Agatha who had caught her. Sister Agatha's eyes were slotted and cold and her mouth so tight and angry it was scarcely more than a thin line on her thin face. One graying lock of red hair had dared to sneak out of the tight knot under Agatha's cap. She jammed it back in place. Then she smoothed her big-knuckled hands over her skirt, a skirt as blue as the berries. "What have you been doing *this* time, you imp of Satan?"

"Nothing."

"Nothing indeed. You dare say that to me, who knows you so well! Secrets again. Secrets are not the Shaker way. I have told you that before, and surely that is an easy thing to remember. Well I can see that your hands have not been at God's work. Nor your mouth. And where your imp's heart has been . . ."

Sarah's stubborn nature, already well-defined at six, had taken over. The answer she returned, though she had not known it then, had already been tried by a succession of stubborn Shaker children. And the answer returned had always been the same.

"I had a gift," said Sarah defiantly. "A gift to . . . to go berrying."

"Oh, a gift to go berrying!" The woman's sarcasm was not lost on the child.

4

Sarah's little heart-shaped chin had jutted out, and her own mouth grew thin. She hid her stained hands behind her back, not daring to have them show up against the white of her apron and further inflame Sister Agatha's well-known temper.

"Yes," she repeated, defiantly flinging herself toward whatever fate was readying to pounce. "A gift to go berrying."

"And I," Sister Agatha said, pouncing, "have a gift to go switching."

She had dragged Sarah, who knew better than to cry out, to a nearby hazel tree. Then she had stripped a switch, lifted Sarah's skirt and petticoat, and birched her little legs seven times for the deadly sins. And then one extra for Sarah's own special sin. Each beat of the switch as it sang with deadly accuracy through the air was accompanied by Sister Agatha's heavy, breathy counting, as if the spoken numbers were all that kept her hand in control.

The pain was less than the shame. Sarah had never quite forgiven Sister Agatha for being so right — and so wrong. And because she had never forgiven Sister Agatha, Sarah had always gone out of her way to be especially loving and good toward her. She sought Sister Agatha out, asking, "Sister Agatha, may I brush your hair?" for it was lovely red-and-white hair, long and heavy, springy and thick. Or "Sister Agatha, my chores are done. May I help you with the dishes?" for she knew that Sister Agatha's hands ached from their long immersion in the water, the big knuckles white with pain against reddened fingers. But Sister Agatha, with a thin-mouthed, angry grunt, always denied needing such help.

5

And Sarah was always sure to set herself twirling faster and faster in Sabbath Meeting so that she might crash into Sister Agatha and hold her clingingly, crying out all the while, "Love, love, love." For then Sister Agatha, weeping and sobbing and shaking, would hold her, too, and whisper into Sarah's ears alone, "Love, love, love."

Sarah did this knowingly, even at six, for she remembered how in the Worldly days, before they had become Shakers, Sister Agatha had been her mother and she had been Sister Agatha's only living child.

Now Sarah gazed again at her scraped hands. The throbbing in them brought her back to the moment. Holy Hill was so far from the main buildings of the Church family that she feared she might have missed hearing the dinner bell in her reverie. Tucking a stray thick russet curl under her cap, and smoothing the pleats of her skirt as she went, Sarah began to run down the path.

She crossed the dirt road and ducked under the split-rail fence. The herb gardens were empty of brethren, their hoes crossed in orderly fashion away from the footpaths. The round and inviting barn seemed empty as well.

Breathing hard, she entered the brick Dwelling House. She heard nothing. It was either broad grace time or — and she hoped she was wrong — everyone was already at the table eating their silent meal. If that was so, she would never be allowed to enter late. After all, she had no excuse. She was supposed to have been running errands for the sisters in the Dyeing and Weaving Shop. No dinner — and she

6

would have to offer some kind of explanation for her tardiness and spend many difficult minutes in extra confession with Eldress Tabit.

Sarah raced around the corner of the women's room and stopped short. Her shoes! Where had she left her shoes and stockings? Surely not on Holy Hill. Her mind went back over her trip. She could not remember taking them off.

Thirty heads were bowed, but Sarah had not stopped in time. A few of the younger girls looked up and saw her. Sister Ann stifled a giggle. Sister Agatha glanced briefly over at Sarah without moving her head. Only her eyes shifted.

Sarah sat down at once at the end of the row of girls. She perched on the edge of the wooden bench and tucked her feet as far back under as they would go. She did not even dare to let her arm touch the sister next to her. That way, perhaps, no one would really notice her unshod feet. But from the corner of her eye she could see Sister Agatha, whose eyes were closed as if in prayer but whose nostrils flared like an angry beast's.

"Love, love, love," Sarah thought desperately at Sister Agatha, but it calmed neither those fierce nostrils nor her own racing heart. She had no time to compose her thoughts before the second dinner bell rang.

Mother Jean and the eldress, Sister Tabit, came into the room. At Mother's signal, the sisters stood in an orderly fashion. Even Sarah managed to tame her fidgeting hands and trembling legs. Eyes straight ahead, they all marched in a mannerly, silent column into the dining hall, where they arranged themselves in their familiar places.

❧ 2. Abel

Brother Abel stood in the well of the round
barn and let the smells flood over him. They
were good, strong smells: earth and spring air,
grain and dung; all part of a great plan of which he
understood only the smallest part. He breathed in
deeply and ran his fingers through his hair.

Abel truly joyed in his work in the stone barn, so
big and so sturdily built that many brethren could
labor in it at the same time and never be in one
another's way. The perfection of their rhythms
seemed a hymn, and Abel would often listen to the
sounds of the others as he worked. Rarely did they
talk. They all knew their jobs too well for comment;
besides, they were encouraged to silence and con-
templation. But the other sounds were the ones that
Abel especially liked: the occasional grunt of a man
or a beast, the soft low of a cow being milked, the
complaining bray of a mule, even the grumblings
overhead as a wagon rolled across the driveway floor.

Abel picked up the pitchfork that had been leaning against him, picked it up and hefted it in his
hands. Instead of starting to work immediately, he
began to turn, slowly at first, letting his eyes set the
barn to spinning. Cows and stanchions whirled past

him. Then the great round ventilator that let steam from the hay rise up and out of the barn went by. Cows, steam, cows, steam; soon they were a blur, a melt of color.

He stopped suddenly, and as his head cleared, the spinning barn slowed. He laughed aloud, but the sound touched only a tiny space in the big stone building.

Whoever had made the first round barn had been truly gifted, Abel thought. Brother Joshua said that round walls kept the devil from hiding in the corners. Abel guessed that corners were not really part of the great plan because what in the world — what in the universe — had corners except when man made it? God's world was round. The sun was round. The moon was round. The earth was round. Trees hewed through were round. Even the body's parts were rounded.

The thought of bodies was an involuntary one. Abel jammed his pitchfork into the wooden floor, shut his eyes, and willed his mind to think of round Shaker things instead. Round hats, round rugs, round boxes nesting together, singing circles, dancing circles, the round stone barn. "To turn and turn will be our delight," he sang to himself, "so that turning, turning, we come round right." But each turning, each circle, brought him around again to the roundness of bodies. He could not keep his mind clean, and his happy mood was gone for good.

Abel had been warned many times that he might be assaulted by these sudden Worldly thoughts. But while a *boy* might have problems in willing away unworthy pictures in his mind, a *man* should have no such trouble. At sixteen, Abel was considered a man, yet he wondered how he *could* be if he was still overruled by his own wicked mind.

"Here, boy, quit turning and mumbling and set to work," called out Brother Joshua. He looked at Abel from under bushy eyebrows and waggled a wooden pitchfork at him, but he smiled.

Glad of the call, Abel nodded toward the older man. He let his fingers idle around the pitchfork's smooth handle for only a moment. Then he pulled it out of the floor and turned to work.

The morning moved swiftly. The spring air, fresh and inviting in the barn, did not tempt Abel from his labors, and the ringing of the first dinner bell came as a surprise. He was slow to put his pitchfork down.

"Come, boy, the body needs food if it is to work efficiently," Joshua called out to him at last. He walked past Abel, pushed past Apostle, a cow near her full term, and went into the tool room, where he set his fork against the stones. Taking down his broad-brimmed hat from its peg, the old man waved Abel on.

There were just the two of them left in the barn. The others had already gone out into the bright spring noon, prompted by the bell. Joshua, slowed by a game leg and a reluctance to leave a job half done, always lagged behind. Most days Abel tarried just to keep Joshua company. Despite the difference in their ages, Brother Joshua was Abel's closest friend. He had been a caretaker in the children's order during some of Abel's first years in New Vale and was now his confessor. And though single, ex-

10

clusive friendships were usually discouraged, this one had had the blessing of the late Father Zebiah, who had seen in it "only the solidarity of innocents," as he had stated many times.

The two walked in silence across the well-kept lawn, Abel fitting his steps to Joshua's limping walk. As a child Abel had once tried to imitate that limp in order to be more like his hero. But Brother Joshua had been quick to cure him of it, making Abel walk half the day with a stick tied tightly to his leg, saying, "That is how it feels to be lamed, lad. 'Tis not comfortable, is it?" And it was not. As Abel remembered that day, he smiled, keeping his eyes on the figures of the other men ahead of them. From the distance they were almost as indistinguishable as strangers, alike in their dark trousers, white shirts, long dark vests, and hats. Yet Abel knew them all. They were his family.

As the last of the brethren turned into the Dwelling House, Abel turned to Joshua. Joshua was the only one he could trust with the trick questions that had plagued him more and more of late. They were not the kind of questions he might bring up in Meeting or in one of the smaller Union groups. They were not the kind of easy questions that Father James could solve with one quick uncompromising sentence. They were, Abel suspected, really unshakerly questions. But Brother Joshua would never tax him with that, nor would he insist in reporting Abel's confession to Elder Eben or to Father James, though, by Shaker laws, he was supposed to.

Not Joshua, who though he had been a Believer for more than twenty years and had signed the covenants giving over all his Worldly goods to the

11

community, had not — as he put it — "given over my tongue as well." Joshua was a Shaker in the flesh but not entirely in the heart, Abel had heard it said. He was not entirely sure what that meant, but he knew that Joshua had no desire for advancement in the community, did not want to become a trustee or an elder. "I like currying horses and cows," the old man had said, "not favor." It had been his answer to Abel's question as to why he was plain Brother Joshua and not Father Joshua, and it was all the answer Abel had ever had from him. He had never dared raise that particular question again. Perhaps — and here Abel gave way to a heretical thought — perhaps Joshua's crusty honesty and his unshakerly heart were what made him the best kind of listener to Abel's awful questions.

"Been thinking," Abel began, clipping his sentences to the length of Joshua's uneven steps. He always began his questions to Brother Joshua that way. It was a kind of special signal between them.

"Not always a good thing, thinking," came Joshua's regular reply.

"About round things," Abel continued. "I have been thinking about round things. Barns being round seems so right."

" 'Tis," replied Joshua.

"But then why . . . why are Worldly barns cornered? Least I have heard it said they are. It seems so simple to me. If round barns are right, then build round barns."

Joshua shook his head. "Things do not always make sense, boy," he said. "Not in the World, surely. And not always here, either. Remember, only this barn in New Vale and the one out in Hancock are round. Even Shakers build barns with corners. And there are some of the World's barns that be round. I know. I saw one once."

"But why?"

Joshua kept walking. "Ask 'em."

"Who can I ask? Younger brothers are not allowed to talk to any Worldly visitors. But there is so much still that I want to understand, so many things I want to know. Why are there not more round barns?" His voice ended on a loud, querulous note.

The old man's face did not change. "Why so much passion over such a small question?" he asked.

"It is *not* a small question," said Abel.

"Father James would say that there are two kinds of questions in the world: small questions and Shaker questions." Joshua looked over at Abel and waggled his eyebrows.

"Well, this is not a Shaker question, I suppose," said Abel slowly. "But it is not exactly a small question either. It is about the World's folk. I just do not understand them."

Joshua nodded and thought a minute. "Could not understand the World's folk then. Do not understand them now. That is why I am here and they are there." His chin indicated a spot beyond the Dwelling House. "And so here I stay. But you, boy, you do not have to stay. Everyone has a choice to make in life. You can always go and ask them the questions yourself. Yo do not have to stay." It was the end of the conversation.

They washed their hands at the pump in silence and went into the Dwelling House. After taking their coats down from the pegs and setting their hats up in the coats' place, they joined the other men and boys already deep in prayer.

As the full silence settled over the room, Abel turned over Joshua's last word. *He did not have to stay.* What an incredible thought. Where else would he go? He was a Shaker. He had always been a Shaker. He did not know any other way. But Brother Joshua's words to him had been, "You do not have to stay." The fifteen minutes of broad grace were not nearly enough time to try to understand them.

Father James, stern and unsmiling, came into the room with Brother Eben behind. He nodded his head smartly, and the brethren stood. Abel, in his turn, filed after the older men while the four brothers who were younger than he came after. They entered the dining room in a perfect line.

The sun filtering through the angled casement windows was as clean and as pure as if it had taken care to wash itself before touching the glass. It laid a broad patina of light across the painted wood sills and the dust-free wide-board floors. Abel silently counted the boards as they walked in, knowing it would be forty-seven steps and the crossing of ten boards before he reached his own place.

The sisters of the community marched in from the opposite door, their shoes tapping out a sure rhythm on the floor. The sound so pleased Abel that he looked down to watch their feet. As the last few entered, he saw with a shock that one of the girls was unshod.

Fascinated, he watched her feet move lightly under the blue of her skirt. Fearfully he let his eyes wander

14

up the dress to her hands. They, at least, were folded in proper Shaker style, modestly, right thumb over the left, on top of the white apron. He looked higher, skipping quickly over the crossed white hand-kerchief on her breast, past her neck, to the heart-shaped face capped in white, where a stray reddish curl threatened to fall over one eye.

She looked frightened, yet somehow defiant. He knew her name. Sara. He had seen her before, though he had never really noticed her. She was part of the family; that was all that had ever been important to know. But why was she barefoot? Had anyone else noticed? He was so busy watching her and asking unanswerable questions that he stumbled into Brother Andrew beside him.

"Sorry," Abel mumbled as Andrew put out a quick hand to steady him.

There was a sharp intake of breath from Father James at the elders' table.

Abel bowed his head, touching his chin to his chest, bit his lip, and kept still. It took all his courage to keep his eyes open. He forced himself to stare at the rise and fall of his own chest.

Father James waited until all the sisters were at their places. Then he gave a signal for prayer. The family knelt, the men at their tables, the women at theirs. The few sisters whose duties kept them in the kitchen knelt for prayers in the doorway.

Abel knelt, too, and prayed. But all he could think of was to pray for forgiveness. He was surprised to find that he did not ask it for himself, but for Sister Sara, who was shoeless and looked so frightened and so fierce.

✑ 3. Sarah

Sarah sat upright at the table, never once daring to slump. A slim girl, she was always being lectured about her posture and this time did not want to call attention to herself. Eating quickly, not even savoring the meat pie and cowslip greens, she finished by Shakering her plate and scraping it clean, setting the knife and fork tidily together, edges toward her, as required.

There, she thought to herself, as neat as any could ask. She folded her hands in her lap and waited silently for the others to finish.

Mother Jean stood and spoke quietly, but her voice carried throughout the dining room and even into the kitchen, where the bustling sisters stilled to listen. Mother Jean always nodded as she talked, as if each word were an agreement with another, unseen, listener. She spoke of the afternoon chores. Nod, nod, nod punctuated her head. When she sat down again, a ray of sunlight lay across her shoulders like a shawl.

Father James stood up in his place, ringed with shadows. "Brethren who work in the upper barn," he began, his voice seeming to come through his nose, "you will leave off barn work and attend to cleanup upon Holy Hill. The day of celebration is fast approaching. We must make the Hill ready."

Sarah remembered suddenly, with an awful clarity, sitting on the ground by the Fountain Stone up on Holy Hill and removing her shoes and stockings. She bit her lip. If the brethren were going to work there, how could she ever rescue her things? For, naughty as her trip alone up the Hill had been, it was no sin. But if her shoes and hose, her intimate apparel, were touched by a man, it would be a sin for her and the unknowing man. And if she should come upon the men on the Hill, a sister alone with so many brethren . . . the sin of *that* fair took her breath away.

Going up Holy Hill had been a kind of exaltation, a hallelujah to spring. And now this. She could feel her eyes begin to fill with tears at the injustice of it, and she set her jaw. Somehow she would have to get there first, before the men. Since her work this afternoon was to help with the labeling of the seed packages and canned goods that were sold to the World's folk, she would need an excuse. She would tell Mother Jean and Eldress Tabit, who were the packagers, that she had to attend to something else, something immediately important. They were very fond of her and would not be expecting her to be telling an untruth. And indeed, she really *did* have to attend to something else, so it was not *such* a lie.

Sarah thought quickly. If she had a rip in her dress, she would have to do something about that at once. Under the table her hands moved along the seams of her skirt and pulled, but the well-sewn dress would not part under such a small pressure.

Father James was still standing. At a nod from him, the men stood, too, pushing their benches back against the wall. Then they filed out of the room.

After the men left, Mother Jean stood and smiled warmly at the women. At her signal they got up, much more silently than the men. The youngest women, Sarah included, set the benches along the wall. Then they all marched out the women's door in a perfect line.

Sarah sought out Mother Jean at once. "I have a rip in my dress," she said breathlessly, holding her hand over what could have been the offending seam and hating herself for the lie. She was careful to keep her voice low, for it was forbidden to make noise in the halls. "I must attend to it before working in the Labeling Room with you."

Mother Jean smiled at her, never looking at the seam. This last year Sarah had grown so much that she and Mother Jean were now eye to eye.

"That you must, dear Sarà," Mother Jean said quietly. "A torn dress wants for modesty. Do not fear to be alone in the sewing room. Sisters Mary and Elizabeth will be there as well." Her bright blue eyes bore into Sarah's. "And you must put on your shoes and stockings. This is the Church family, not the children's order, after all. You are no longer a child who might come barefoot to dinner."

Sarah bit her lip again and looked at the floor, but Mother Jean patted her on the shoulder and moved serenely on, nodding at several of the older sisters. She never looked back.

Sarah walked partway down the hall toward the sewing room until the last of the sisters disappeared out the door. She glanced back over her shoulder. The hallway was empty. She turned around and raced to the women's door on tiptoe and peered out into the sunlight. She could see a few of the brothers going toward the mill and three more already turning into the orchard. Old Brother Eben, the elder, walking heavily with his stick, was just entering the Brethren's Shop, where he was in charge of the broom making. The men who were to go up Holy Hill were not in sight. Sarah guessed that they were in the barn gathering their tools.

She watched as Mother Jean and Sister Tabit stood by the Herb House door, talking about the gardens. They pointed at first one section, then another, Mother Jean nodding at every statement. At last they went inside.

Sarah waited a moment more, took a deep breath, then stepped out. She ran around the corner of the building, across the prickly beginnings of the new lawn, over the dirt road, and onto the winding, tree-lined path to Holy Hill. She never noticed Sister Agatha's pinched face staring at her from a kitchen window. All Sarah cared about was finding her shoes and stockings up on the hill before the men arrived. If she could get back to the Dwelling House without being seen, she vowed she would never again hold a secret in her heart.

Yet even as she ran, spring seduced her again. Her eyes took in buds like green buttons on the trees. Her ears identified birds. She whispered out loud the names she had given them, for the naming of wild birds had not been in any of the lessons of a Shaker schoolroom. She heard "cheepster" and "smudge" and then smiled as a brilliant flash of the blue "thief bird" flew across her path, screeching.

Halfway up the hill, where the trees gave out and the bushes really began, she turned off the path for a moment to follow a rabbit that loped away from her in a wonderful zigzag pattern.

It was just as well, for as she crouched, watching the rabbit's tail bobbing through the brush, she heard footsteps and voices coming up the path behind her. The men had been faster than she thought.

Not daring to be caught, and fearing the blue of her dress and the white of her neckerchief and cap would give her away, Sarah went farther from the path and undid her cap strings. She snatched the white muslin cap from her head and tucked it into her bodice. Her skirts snagged on a patch of briers but, giving no thought to rips in her haste, she yanked them free. Even the thorns scratching her legs did not slow her down. She only hoped that the men, bent on their mission, would not notice her.

Finding a thicket that looked bushy enough to hide in, she scrambled around it and huddled down as low as she could, bending over to keep the white neckerchief from showing. Modesty alone kept her from removing it as well. She never felt the thorns that pulled at her hair or scratched at her hands. Holding her breath, Sarah hunched her shoulders. She began to shiver, and she could feel her heart thudding somewhere high up in her chest.

"Dear God," she prayed silently, and then could think of nothing further to say. She felt that at any minute a hand would descend on her shoulder — a man's hand — and that she would be found, and they would both be damned.

The voices moved farther up the hill and at last Sarah dared to look up, craning her neck to see around the bushes. There was no one in sight. Still in a crouched position, she crept from behind the thicket. She fished the cap from her bodice and put it back on her head, neglecting, in her haste, to push all the stray curls under. She could no longer go up to get her shoes and stockings. Now the men would find them for sure. She bit her lip at the thought. Standing, she lifted her skirts above her knees, modesty giving way to speed, and ran down the hill. As she ran, tears streamed down her face, and she began, raggedly, to count her sins:

> One, coming on Holy Hill.
> Two, being late to broad grace.
> Three, losing stockings and shoes.
> Four, lying to the Mother.
> Five, returning to the Hill.
> Six, being unable to pray.
> Seven . . .

"Ruining your clothes again. You are the *most* sinful, unnnatural child born of woman. And *this* for the sin of being born into the World," screamed Sister Agatha, grabbing Sarah as she passed the kitchen door. The spoon in Agatha's hand seemed to whine as it descended on Sarah's shoulders and arms, finishing the work of the thorns.

Over and over the spoon rained down on her, and

Sarah could do nothing but put her hands up to protect her head and scream.

Agatha was stopped at last by the kitchen sisters and by Mother Jean and Sister Tabit who, upon hearing Sarah's hysterical screams, came running out of the Herb House. They took several blows themselves from the wooden spoon, and Sister Tabit's nose was bloodied, before they could separate Agatha from her weapon and send the weeping, shaking Sarah upstairs in the Dwelling House to the room called the Nurse Shop.

Sarah went up the stairs slowly, leaning on Mother Jean's arm, but she would have liked to run up the steps two at a time to get away from the hateful, hurting words that followed her upstairs.

"Imp! Devil! *Satan's child!*" Sister Agatha was still calling after her, and the message echoed in Sarah's mind. She wondered if she would ever forget the sound.

Sitting on a bed in the Nurse Shop, stripped to her shift with a blanket around her, Sarah sat silently while Mother Jean sponged her upturned face. At last she was able to murmur through a tight throat, "Sister Agatha's hand is hard."

Mother Jean finished cleansing Sarah's wounds, her head nodding at the thorn scratches on Sarah's legs and feet. She made no mention of them. She took the blanket from Sarah's shoulders and pushed her gently but firmly down onto the bed. Just as she finished tucking the blanket around Sarah's body, Mother Jean offered a single short sentence.

"God's hand is harder," she said, and left the room.

❧ 4. Abel

Abel, Brother Joshua, and four other men gathered in the barn. The hoes and cutters were lined up precisely in the tool room, honed and polished. Each man chose a set of tools, and Abel carried a rake. The youngest of the work party, he would do the cleanup.

As they walked up the hill, Abel kept silent. To doubly insure that he would not find himself chattering, he strode ahead. Behind he could hear the others talking. Even Brother Joshua made a small joke about the weather.

Usually the ascent up Holy Hill, whether for work or for worship, melted away Abel's Worldly thoughts. Just the act of setting his feet on the path was enough to turn him right. But this day the sun seemed to ride between his shoulders. It burned into his bones. He wondered briefly if he was feverish. He was never sick; it was his one source of real pride — his health. But the burning continued, and he thought suddenly of fierce-frightened Sara.

As her heart-shaped face came unbidden into his mind, the fever peaked. He felt it simultaneously on his cheeks as if he wore a brand there, and shooting pains in his legs. Momentarily he felt weak and stumbling. He took a deep breath and forced himself to walk faster up the hill. If this was a sickness, he would conquer it.

As always, the hilltop took his breath away. In the middle of a wilderness, marked only by a trodden path through trees and scrub-brush, was a place of man-made peace. The square, seeded lawn was already showing the promise of green beauty. The carefully hewn fence was at once upright and plain. A proper Shaker fence, he reminded himself. And in the center of the fence the Fountain Stone.

Abel walked up to the fence and read again, as he had twice a year every year since he could remember, the words carved into the marble:

> *Written and placed here by the command*
> *of our Lord and Saviour* . . .

His mouth moved as he read, but no sound came out. He closed his eyes and savored the words. He savored as well the idea that God should care so much for the Shakers that He commanded them to build Him a special, secret, sacred place. And what a further blessing, Abel thought, that he, Abel, was allowed — even commanded — to help caretake such a holy.

He opened his eyes and walked around to the far side to read the inscription on the stone's back, letting his fingers trail along the fence.

By the back end of the fence were a pair of shoes, a woman's shoes, with two stockings trailing off from them. One of the shoes lay on its side, and the stockings still held the slight bulge of the owner's calves.

The sight should have startled him, horrified him with its sacrilege. But somehow he had already known that he would find them there. *Her* shoes. *Her* stockings. And finding them at the Fountain Stone consecrated them in his mind.

The sun hit him full in the face then, nearly blinding him. It was a sure sign, he thought. A gift. He dropped the rake and knelt down, touching the overturned shoe with the tip of one finger. It was all he could dare.

"Sara," he whispered, remembering her small feet moving lightly under the blue skirt, tiptoeing across the wide boards. The burning began again on his face, in his chest, between his legs. "Sara," he said again, savoring the heat. "Sara."

He reached out tentatively toward one of the stockings but in the end could not bring himself to touch it. For a long moment he stared at the stocking. At the rounded shape of it. Lying on the greening ground, it seemed so innocent. Yet he knew what the others would say about such a sinful thing. He could not touch it. "Dear God," he whispered, praying for strength, and reached out once more.

At that, he heard the voices of the others making the last turn before the top. Without thinking out the why of it, he stripped off his coat, put his hands back into the sleeves and gathered up the stockings and shoes. He wrapped them solidly in the jacket's folds, never letting his naked skin touch them. Briefly he smelled something foreign to him. It was neither spring air nor ground smell. He tightened his lips together, set the coat neatly to one side of the fence, and was up and rolling up his shirt sleeves by the time the other brethren arrived.

"He lusts for work, that boy," said Brother Frank, who was never without his long-stemmed clay pipe. The others laughed companionably and took off their own coats, setting them in an orderly row by Abel's. Brother Frank took a minute to light his pipe, and then they all began the necessary pruning and cleaning that would make the clearing ready for the coming mountain feast.

Work went easily on the hilltop grounds; the years of prideful caretaking made the labor simple. By the time the ghostly echo of the supper bell reached them, the men were finished with their work. They picked up their coats. Only Abel lagged behind.

"Are you coming, boy?" asked Brother Frank, waving his pipe in Abel's direction. "Your work is finished, too."

The others murmured agreement. Brother Joshua cocked his head to one side and stared at Abel, as if suddenly seeing him in a different light.

"I will be along in a moment," Abel said, surprised at the ease with which the words slipped out. He needed the brethren down the hill and out of sight before he dared take the . . . things . . . out of his coat. "I would look around once again."

Joshua grunted. "No need to explain," he said. "Only the guilty offer explanations."

"Guilty!" Brother Frank exploded with laughter at such an idea. The others laughed with him. Then the thought of food after the long afternoon of out-

26

door work claimed their attention. No one but Joshua noticed Abel's sudden interest in the ground. Following Brother Frank's lead, they started down the hill.

Joshua was last. He stood for a moment to stare at Abel. Then, giving a quick nod, he went down the hill, limping after the others.

Abel did not even dare nod back. Instead he pretended to walk around the hilltop as if seeking out rough places, untidy places that only he could manage. He felt the falseness in his every step. But as soon as Brother Joshua limped around the first turn, Abel walked back to his coat.

Standing over it, he thought he smelled once again the musky unfamiliar smell of the stockings. He knelt down and, as if unwrapping a gift, unfolded the coat. He did not know what he expected to find. The shoes and stockings lay there, jumbled together, but the magic was gone from them. They were simply a pair of shoes and stockings. One stocking was neatly darned near the toe. One shoe was badly scuffed at the heel. He bundled them back up in his coat, being careful not to touch them with his hands. Then he picked up the rake and walked slowly down Holy Hill.

It had turned cold, and clouds covered the sun. His shoulders ached, less from the work, which he was used to, than from holding himself as if waiting for a blow. It seemed a long way back to the Dwelling House, though the turnings in the path were all familiar ones. All the way down, he followed only one thought. Somehow he would have to find Sister Sara and tell her that he had discovered her shoes and hose, but that he would keep her terrible secret. It would not be easy. Shaker boys and girls, Shaker men and women were never allowed to be alone together, to touch one another, or to speak to one another about personal things. It was the *most* important rule. But he *would* find her, somehow. Find her and tell her — and be done with it.

☙ 5. Sarah

In the Nurse Shop Sarah slipped into an uneasy sleep in which she dreamed she was being pecked by birds who screamed at her in an unknown tongue. When she awoke, the afternoon was full of shadows.

Mother Jean walked quietly into the room, the tip-tap of her feet on the floor a comforting rhythm. She nodded but said nothing to Sarah, tucking the covers in even more tightly than before and putting her hand for several moments on Sarah's forehead.

Sarah tried to sit up. She wanted to talk about the beating. She thought that if she confessed to Mother Jean about the things that had led up to Sister Agatha's attack, the viciousness of the attack might make some sense to her. But Mother Jean would not let her speak. Each time Sarah tried to open her mouth, Mother's roughened hand came over it.

"Hush, hush, child," Mother Jean said soothingly, pushing Sarah back down. "It is not yet time to talk of it. You have a wordy heart."

But Sarah could not be soothed. She ached in too many places, and the tight covers rubbed her arms and shoulders like sandpaper. Where the briers had scratched her legs, she could feel little rivers of fire. She tried once more to speak.

Mother Jean clucked her tongue and shook her head. "This is not time for confession," she remonstrated. "This is time for silence. The answers to questions come only in silence. If you talk too loudly, how can you hear what God is saying?" Her nodding head punctuated each sentence. Then she smiled and stood up. Her standing eased the pressure on the covers, and Sarah sighed out loud. "But," cautioned Mother Jean, "if you do not learn to listen, my child . . ." and then she was gone, taking the silence with her.

As soon as Mother Jean was out of the room, Sarah's head began to burst with noisy questions. She squirmed and tossed, and soon the bedding was in a tangle around her. All her training cried out to her to get out of bed and straighten it again. But once out, standing and shivering in her cotton undergarment, Sarah could no longer bear to climb back, even though her shoulders and arms ached. She bent over suddenly and smoothed the dark quilt with short, sharp strokes.

When she stood and straightened her shoulders, she almost savored the pain of her back, probing it like a loose tooth, now to feel the aching, now to feel the pleasure of the pain's release. She *did* have a wordy heart, but perhaps silence was Mother Jean's way — not hers.

Sarah looked around the Nurse Shop, suddenly aware that it was in this very room, not five months past, that old Sister Lucy had departed this life. She had gone in silence, lying in an oversized wooden cradle, with a peculiar smile on her lips. Every sister had taken a turn with her, rocking the cradle and bringing water or blackberry leaf tea to her when she cried out, rubbing a poultice of pennywort and cream on her cracked lips. For weeks the sisters had all imitated Sister Lucy's smile in Meeting, rocking back and forth as if in a cradle, and singing a song that Sister Tabit taught them. It was a little gift of song given to her by Sister Lucy one night not a week after she had died. The refrain popped into Sarah's head:

> *In Zion's clean and holy land*
> *We smile and smile and smile.*

But Sarah was not smiling as she tiptoed, dress and cap in hand, out of the room and into the long, empty hall.

She felt feverish and lightheaded, and she walked as if into a dreamscape. Light from the opened bedroom doors streamed in from the west side, marking the polished floor like a newly furrowed field. Little dust motes danced in the rays. For a moment Sarah wanted to take each ray and give it a good shake to clean it. She shook her head instead. The movement caused other motes, spots of light, to dance before her eyes.

As she went farther down the hall, she was aware for the first time in her life how perfect the Dwelling House was and how like a dream. Nothing was out of place. It was as preserved as a tomb. She felt unaccountably sad and, at the same time, wanted to scream out. She had never been alone during an afternoon since becoming a Shaker. Not once, alone, up on the empty second floor. And in her undergarment where anyone might see her. Somehow she did not care. Modesty had deserted her completely, and no other virtue, it seemed, was ready to rush in to fill its place.

Her feet found the lines of the floorboards, and she could feel the ridges impress on her soles. She put one foot in front of the other, slowly, following the straight lines until she came to her own sleeping room. It was the second from the end. She stepped just inside the door.

She looked around her room as if she had never seen it before, as if she were suddenly staring into a room that belonged to someone else. The four painted wooden bedsteads hugging the walls were tidily made up. Not a wrinkle marred the surfaces of the matching blue-and-white wool quilts. From the blue pegboard along the walls hung four ladderback chairs and the cloaks and bonnets of each girl. The folds of the cloaks fell in exactly the same way. Sabbath shoes, well polished, were placed neatly below each cloak. Between the beds, side by side, were two double chests. A single small looking glass hung over one chest. A towel rack bearing four white linen towels stood by another chest. Four candleholders and two white stoneware water pitchers and bowls were atop the chests. Inset in the east walls, on either side of the doorway, were six wooden drawers filled with fresh undergarments and bed linen.

Sister Elizabeth's basket of sewing was on a small candlestand by her bed. Sister Mary's candlestand held a Bible and a pair of spectacles. She could not read without them. Sister Ann's candlestand bore a round box, which was filled with dream messages. Ann received all kinds of dream gifts at night and conscientiously wrote them down when she awoke, but she had yet to share them aloud with anyone at Meeting. Sarah assumed she had confessed them to Sister Tabit. Those dream messages were not considered secrets, only not-quite-finished gifts. Sarah's own candlestand held the girls' glass lamp. As the youngest members of the Church family, the four girls had to share. It was not that the family lacked the means, but learning to share, learning to do without, learning to value the simple life, was part of the Shaker way.

Looking at the perfect room, Sarah had a sudden memory of another room, small, crowded, and smoky. It seemed filled to the bursting with things: a ragdoll in a cradle, a chest overflowing with blankets, a niddy noddy half-strung with yarn, a pair of dirty boots lying on the hearth, a ginger cat asleep by the fire. And two sounds: a woman crooning a low lullaby and the voice of a laughing man. As quickly, the memory left her, without a glimpse of the man's face or the words of the woman's song, and Sarah wondered if it, too, had been a dream, though it was a waking dream she had had before.

She stepped another foot inside the door and

gasped. It was more than the ache in her shoulders, the dull throbbing of her arms, the tiny fires along her scratched legs. She was suddenly aware that she was the only part of the picture that was not perfect. Throwing her dress and cap onto her bed, glorying in new sharp pains that the motion sent along her back, Sarah walked over to the curtained window.

She saw several sisters laboring in the herb garden. Beyond them lay the round barn, a comfortable-looking structure. She had never been inside. Barn work was men's work, though several of the older sisters were allowed in to do the spring milking. She thought it might be nice to stroke a milch cow, to feel its velvety nose and have its hot breath blow upon her hands. She wondered, only briefly, how she knew that feel. It, too, seemed a part of the small, smoky dream world, the world of the crooning woman and the laughing man.

As she stood watching, the first supper bell rang. By twos and threes, the brethren and sisters came from their work places and walked with sure, unhurried steps toward the Dwelling House, stopping only to wash their hands at the pump. Long after they had disappeared into the building, one of the younger brothers came, hurrying, his coat clutched in his arms. Sarah watched him disapprovingly. He must be wrinkling his coat. Here was another who was spoiling the perfect Shaker picture. He glanced around, then knelt by a bush and shook out his coat. There was something furtive in his movements. Sarah could not decipher it. Something tumbled from the coat to the ground, but before she could see what it was, he had pushed it under the bush with his foot.

Then he rose and brushed his coat with his hand, both inside and out, as if savoring the feel. His obvious emotion made Sarah blush.

She put her hands up to her hot cheeks, and one elbow touched the curtain. Perhaps the movement of the curtain caught his eye or perhaps it was accidental, but at that moment he looked up and saw her.

Suddenly conscious that she was all but unclothed, as naked as any Jezebel, Sarah shrank away from the glass. Then, biting her lip and defying modesty for the third time that day, she moved to the window and stared back at him.

She was surprised at the violence of his reaction. He threw himself to his knees, hands together in prayer. Then he put his hands up over his face. She could not tell if he was weeping, laughing, or trembling with the sin of seeing a sister undressed. She had expected, at the most, that he would turn quickly away so as not to shame them both. She realized at last that she had shamed herself by what had occurred.

Feeling altogether weak, she sat down on Sister Ann's bed. Every inch of her skin now seemed to be burning. Afraid to stand up near the window, afraid to be seen once more, she got on her hands and knees and crawled along the floor toward her own bed, where her clothes lay in a jumble. In her hurry she bumped against Ann's candlestand, and it began to tip over. She grabbed for it and righted it, but not before the box fell off and onto the floor As the box hit, its top popped off and the small pieces of Ann's paper dreams scattered.

Sarah scrabbled to pick them up, and as she was putting them back into the box, one caught her eye.

It said, "The Valley, the Valley, love in the Valley."
Without meaning to — exactly — she read another.
"Cleanse the Sanctuary. Keep it clean" was its
scrawl. She picked up a third paper. It was crushed
into a tiny crinkled ball. As she smoothed it out,
she saw that it was a list of names decorated with
hearts and doves: "Abel, Andrew, Jacob, Jonas,
John."

Sarah read them in a whisper to herself. "Abel,
Andrew, Jacob, Jonas, John." All at once she
realized that the list named all the young brethren
who had entered adulthood in the last few years,
moving over from the children's order to the Church
family.

"Abel, Andrew, Jacob, Jonas, John, indeed," she
said self-righteously, shoving the rest of the papers
back into the box and closing the lid. But when she
placed the box back on the candlestand, never moving from her sitting position on the cold floor, Sarah
felt a laugh starting and she could not control it.

"Abel, Andrew, Jacob, Jonas, John," she whispered, in between fits of laughter. Sister Ann, who
talked all the time about purity of thought, had been
dreaming about the *brethren*. Even she, Sarah, who
had been wanting for modesty, who had secrets not
confessed, who had left her shoes and hose upon
Holy Hill and been beaten as an imp of Satan, even
she would never dare such a silly, wicked, unshakerly
thing.

"Oh, Sister Ann," said Sarah. "I wonder what you
call *your* gift!"

Then she stood up and threw herself with a whoop
onto her own bed, heedless now of the window or
the pains in her body. Face down on the pillow, she

tried to stop her laughter. After a moment she turned over. Lying on her back, looking at the ceiling, so whitewashed and unseamed, she asked herself at last, "And *my* gift. What is it?"

She smiled again, at Ann's dream gifts and her own outrageousness. She was still smiling when the second dinner bell rang. She did not leave the bed. Instead she watched as the sun, setting behind the barn, flooded the room with reds that rainbowed onto the pure white ceiling and faded, very slowly, into night.

❧ 6. Abel

Slowly Abel put down his hands and stood up. The angelic figure in the window was no longer there. Clad in white, shimmering, a kind of aura around its head, it had appeared suddenly. As suddenly it was gone. Was it a gift? And if so, what kind?

Abel's hands were moist, and he wiped them along the sides of his claret-colored pants. Then, drawing a deep breath, he persuaded his legs toward the pump. Once there, he pumped vigorously, letting the water spill out in a foaming rush. He washed his hands three times, examining them thoroughly between each washing for dirt under the nails or grass stains or some deeper stains he dared not name. At last he was satisfied and put on his coat.

The second supper bell rang. The very ordinariness of the sound brought him back to himself. He drew in another breath and went in.

But when he sat down in the dining hall, he could feel the closeness of the women's tables, and hunched his shoulders against them. He ate quickly but never attended to what was on his plate. Only when Mother Jean began to speak did he look up. He was almost surprised to find himself at his customary place, his plate neatly Shakered, with the bones set to one side, the knife and fork together. The meal was at an end. He rose when the others rose. He walked when they walked. If anyone had asked him about the supper, he could not have said what he had eaten.

In the hallway Brother Andrew was the first to speak. Turning to Abel, he whispered, "Apostle will be calving soon. Brother Amos is looking for it any day now. The full moon draws them out. He says I can help."

"A baby," Brother John said to no one in particular. His voice was louder than it should have been, his big, foolish smile spreading wide. "A baby."

"Oh, enough," Jonas snapped at him. Then, seeing Andrew's frown, he added gently, "You are a baby yourself. Come on then, we have to get to our chores."

Abel listened to them squabble. It was a familiar-enough sound. Andrew was usually the peacemaker; Jonas the snappish one who frequently confessed to his temper; Jacob a sullen worker; John the simple saint. Abel wondered how he fit in.

"Coming, Abel?" It was Andrew.

He shook his head. He had no chores that evening, having been on the Holy Hill work party. The emptiness stretched ahead of him. It was almost an hour before retiring time. All at once it was terrifying. He watched the brethren go out the door.

Down the hall, near the women's doorway, a small knot of the younger women were talking in whispers. Unwillingly, his eyes were drawn to them, seeking out Sara, but she was not there.

One girl was gesturing animatedly with her hands. Her moving fingers mesmerized him. Suddenly the hall was unbearably hot. Abel turned abruptly on his heel, pushed through the men's door, and went out into the cool evening air. He *would* help the others, though it was not his assigned task.

Walking purposefully toward the barn, Abel put as much distance as he could between himself and the house. He felt the upstairs windows were alien eyes boring into his back. When he stopped to turn and glare at them, they were as unlit, as unseeing as empty sockets.

He continued into the barn. Evening milking would be done by Andrew, Jonas, and John. It came to him that Brother John would always be a perfect Shaker. His head would never hold a single unseemly question. John would accept angels at a second-story window as readily as devils.

But Abel knew, with sudden surprising clarity, that he himself could not. He was sure now that the figure at the window had been no angel. It had been Sister Sara. She had shown herself to him in an angel's guise until he was ready to understand. *That* was the gift. And the touch of her — he felt her skin already under his fingertips, soft and warm — would be holy and consecrated.

Afire with this revelation, Abel told himself that he would reveal his gift of love to her in Meeting. Surely she would be there to receive it. No one missed Meeting unless they were sick enough for nursing. Ever.

"Evening, Abel." There was a pause, and then the greeting was repeated. "I said, 'Evening, Abel.' "

Abel started. He had not even heard the first greeting. "Evening," he mumbled back.

The speaker was Brother Joshua. He was carrying a kerosene lamp. "Your feet seem to be wandering as much as your head today. Have you come to give me a hand, boy?"

"A hand?" Abel felt as simple as Brother John.

"With the afternoon's tools. I mean to clean and sharpen them."

Glad of something specific to do, Abel followed Brother Joshua into the dark recesses of the barn.

Joshua ground the last edge of the last hoe on the spinning stone. The flickering lamplight made shadows romp along the wall. The hum of the stone and a single cow's lowing were the only sounds. Abel concentrated on the cycles the stone made. It was stopped abruptly by Joshua's gnarled hand.

"I do appreciate the quiet, boy, but you have been unnaturally so. Care to talk about what ails you?" he asked casually. "Confess to your old caretaker?"

Abel shook his head.

Joshua mused. "Spring is a time of quickening, boy. It gets into the blood. Even being a Shaker cannot always stop that. But it can be tamped down and made to grow again in an orderly Shaker way. If that is what you want . . ."

If that was what he wanted? All he wanted was to be a good Shaker. A righteous, hardworking Believer. But then, shaking his head, Abel admitted that he wanted that and something more. Suddenly he found himself pouring out his tale. Of the shoes and stockings, and the angel at the glass. He could not stop the flow of words. They gushed from him. When he finished, he looked up, expecting to see Brother Joshua scowling. Instead the old man's face was thoughtful, serious, his head nodding.

"You know . . ." Joshua began, looking briefly at the ceiling. Abel followed his look. He saw nothing but some pieces of hay that had somehow drifted through the boards and caught on the beams. "You know," Joshua said again, as if reminding himself, "I have never said this to a single soul before. Never thought my life in the World important enough to confess, I guess. But I was in love once. Or thought I was. About your age. The girl was a neighbor girl, maybe two, three years older than I. Quick she was. Full of the spring jimjams. She promised all kinds of delights. We coupled one night. Like horses in the field. She showed me how and she knew a lot, that gal. Had plenty of practice before me. It was sweaty work. Done in a moment. She drowned herself not long after. For love, they said. Not love of me. I knew that even then. I think I could have stood it if it had been for love of me. I wanted the blame, you see. Wanted to be the reason. But a lot of my neighbors were quicker to claim the blame. That spring the boys all wore her death on their sleeves more

40

openly than they had ever worn her love. So I kept still, and none of them ever knew I had had a part in it. But I never wanted another girl again. A moment of sweaty pleasure is not worth a lifetime of regrets."

Abel looked down at his hands. He found it hard to believe that Brother Joshua had never talked of this before, this most important thing in his life. Confession was urged on them all; it was a cornerstone of the faith. But Joshua would not care about that. Not Brother Joshua. Sweaty pleasure, Joshua had said. Abel remembered his moist palms and how he had drowned the evidence of them at the pump. Was that what Joshua meant?

"It is not like that," Abel said. "Not the spring jimjams. It is not like that at all."

"Then what *is* it like, boy?" asked Joshua softly. "In all your telling of it, you told me the what but not the why of it."

Abel was silent for a moment. "I do not know," he said at last. "It just happened. There *is* no why of it."

"And what will you do?" Joshua asked. "Shout it out in Meeting?"

"I thought . . ." Abel began, ready to explain that this had been his intention. But Joshua's saying it out loud made such a plan seem stupid or, what was worse, trivial.

"Or will you confess it in private to Father James?" Joshua's voice held the slightest note of contempt. "The prize stonethrower who is totally without sin."

"Father James? But he . . ." Abel's voice trailed

off once again. He was incapable of guessing the kind of punishment Father James would dream up. It would be something humiliating and very suitable. He was known for that. Like the time he had punished old Brother Abram, who had been a trustee and had lost New Vale a lot of money buying suckling pigs that were diseased. Abram had been forced to eat with the dying piglets for a week. Some said he had died of a broken heart. That he had been buried secretly in the pigpen. Others said that the shame was so great he had run away into the World and died in a home for drunkards. Abel did not know the truth of the ending. All he knew was that Brother Abram had been there one day and gone the next.

Abel put his hand on the grindstone. He turned it, needing to hear once again its comforting whir. "A father *should* punish his children if they have offended."

Brother Joshua stopped the wheel and spoke slowly into the silence. "I do not know what a father *should* do, never having been a father myself," he said. "But I know what *I* would do."

"What?"

"I would remind you that it was spring. And that there is a mighty lot of work in any spring for young hands to do." Joshua held out his hand and Abel grabbed hold of it.

Pulling the old man up, Abel was surprised to see that his own hand was bigger by a knucklesworth. He had always thought of Brother Joshua as a large man, a mountain. When had he shrunk?

Joshua limped over to the wall and set the hoe

down. He took the lantern from the wall hook. "Retiring time, I would guess. Time to learn to hold your tongue. And guard your heart, boy."

They walked out together, matching step for step back to the brick dwelling House and up the stairs to their rooms.

🍂 7. Meeting

The silence in the Dwelling House was a ripe, palpable presence. In their resting rooms the seventy members of the Church family sat erect, hands folded to pray away the requisite half-hour of retiring time.

Brother Frank, lulled by the full meal at the end of the long workday, dozed off without his habitual stuttering snores. Joshua, who was his roommate, poked him awake, and Brother Frank stood and bowed four times as was required, then sat down again, smiling sheepishly at Joshua.

In his own room Abel did not pray. Instead, he went over and over the words that Brother Joshua had spoken to him in the barn. If spring was indeed a time of quickening, then perhaps that was what he felt, only that. But the image of the horses coupling in the field kept troubling him. He could not imagine human beings in such a position. His thoughts continued to bother him the rest of the time, but they did not seem to communicate themselves to the others. Jacob and Jonas, hands folded, were their usual unsmiling selves. Andrew had a peaceful smile that played around his mouth. His eyelids fluttered open and shut at intervals. Only Brother John was grinning broadly. He sat with his feet caught around the legs of his chair. His pale blue, watery eyes were open and staring. As a child, he had once volunteered that he often saw God and Mother Ann eating apple pie when he prayed. His grin probably meant he was seeing another such vision.

In Sarah's room all movement was slowed. Bible in her lap, black-skinned Mary followed the lines of text with a laggard finger. Her glasses, perched on her broad nose, seemed ready to fall off. Elizabeth and Ann, clothed in identical expressions of piety, breathed heavily, as if laboring mightily at their prayers. Ann had darted one quick, angry look at Sarah when the girls first entered the room, stooping to pick up a piece of paper from under her bed. Sarah had started, seeing it, knowing it to be one of the spilled paper dreams she had missed. She hoped that Ann would not suspect her. But whom else could Ann blame? After all, it was Sarah who had been alone in the room. They had found her dressed and waiting, with her Sabbath shoes feeling tight and uncomfortable on her feet. She had been sitting upright and unmoving on her chair because it was the only way to keep her back and shoulders from hurting. Ann had said nothing, hiding the crumpled paper quickly in her pocket. Sarah thought again about Ann's basket and about the kneeling brother on the lawn. And then she saw once more, as if in another waking dream, the smoky room filled with worn objects; heard again the bright, bold laughter of the unseen man and the deep, throaty croon of the woman's lullaby.

In the room she shared with Sister Ruth, Agatha would not let herself move. She knew if she moved before the bell her sins would be redoubled. Clenching her hands till the fingers first burned hot, then lost all sensation, she tried to pray. But Sarah's face kept intruding. That beautiful young face, fresh with spring, and the smile that was his. *His.* That face was a constant reminder of the time when she had longed to be embraced. Embraced by Satan. She knew he was Satan. By the gap between his front teeth. It was the sure sign of the sybarite. The sensualist. And Sara's smile was the same. She must not be led down that same path. Already Sara was of the age when Agatha had been taken. Corrupted. Used. Worn. But here at New Vale they had both been given another start, a chance to become angels. To live uncorrutible lives. They were sisters now. *Sisters.* But surely a sister had as much right here as a mother to chastise a child. She would beat the sensualist out of Sara for her own good, that they both might be saved. Agatha's fingers tingled, signaling that she had relaxed her work-roughened hands too much. She tightened them again. If they were bruised in the morning, she would know her prayers were being answered.

Mother Jean in her private room rocked back and forth on the straight-backed cane rocker. Eyes closed, lips set firmly together, she thought about Sister Agatha, who was probably sitting rigidly in the next room. What unconfessed secrtes, Mother Jean wondered, fueled the fires of Agatha's fierce heart? For Mother Jean was sure that only a hidden sin — perhaps even hidden from Agatha herself — could make such a hardworking sister prey to such ungovernable rages, such changes in mood. She remembered when Agatha had arrived nearly ten years before, an anxious, needful young widow with a beautiful red-haired child clinging to her hand. She had seemed troubled, but certainly not deranged — or they would never have taken her in. It was not Shaker policy to minister to the crazed, for each brother and sister had to pull his or her own weight within the community. But sorrowing folk were always welcome. She herself had flown to the Believers on the wings of pain. Work, Mother Jean knew full well, could ease a troubled life. And Sister Agatha had seemed to fit in easily, giving up her child to the care of the children's order without a moment's regret, adjusting to calling the little girl sister, instead of daughter, far sooner than most. Only now . . . now that Sister Sara was growing into a woman gifted with an appealing, high-spirited character, Sister Agatha seemed troubled again, changed. As Mother to the Church family, Mother

Jean knew she would have to find a path to understanding for them all. But not this moment. Not . . .
now. Now was the time for prayer. Dismissing Sister
Agatha from her mind, Mother Jean settled quickly
into a silent, fruitful dialogue with her God.

In his solitary quarters Father James stood. His
hands were over his eyes as if shielding them from
the sight of evil. He was as rigorous as any prophet
in seeking out sins in others. It was for this, he knew,
that he had been sent as a boy to New Vale when
his parents had died. He had known from the
beginning that he was to be the Father of New Vale
one day. He had striven toward it with all his might,
secretly scourging himself at night to purify his body,
testing himself so that he would not be found wanting when the time came. He wore his shining right-
eousness like a coat of armor, knowing he was God's
appointed knight, Mother Ann Lee's champion. If
his prayers were more like demands, that was only
between himself and God.

The bell sounded, putting an abrupt end to retiring time. The Believers stood and marched out of
their rooms, the last in each group blowing out the
candles. In orderly columns, two abreast, as solemn
as the animals filing into the Ark, they went down
the separate stairways. Men with men, women with
women, they marched into the dining hall. The tables
and chairs had been put away. The wooden benches
were lined up against the walls. In the glow of
the lamplights the well-polished floor gleamed an
invitation.

The creaking floorboards, the tap-tapping of feet, the soft hiss of the dining hall stove — for spring nights were still quite chilly — were all that broke the silence. The men entered the hall first and bowed. They found their places on the wooden benches. Across the room the women entered and did the same.

Wood crackled in the stove. Brother John shuffled his feet until Andrew quieted him. Benches groaned as bodies shifted. Sister Ann sniffled quietly. Sister Mary, remembering suddenly, took off her glasses, putting them in a pocket and tapping the pocket comfortably. Sister Tabit cleared her throat with three small, dry coughs. Hand to nose, Sister Ann sniffled again. Old Brother Eben gave a soft, phlegmy "Harrumph." Then the silence covered them all.

Sarah wondered at the silence. It had never seemed so complete before. And frightening. She wondered if she dared break into it. She thought about what she might say. If she could, like the sisters of fifteen years before, she would speak in another language: Indian or Chinese. Those sudden gifts of unknown tongues had always fascinated her. There was something so wonderfully secret about them. She tried out one of the old gift songs in her head.

> *Quo we lorezum quini*
> *qui qwini qwe qwini qwe*
> *Hock a nick a hick nick . . .*

But it was no use. It could mean anything — or nothing. She wondered if it was sense or nonsense. How did one *really* know if one had a gift of tongues?

48

Or any gift at all? She tried to stop thinking about anything, just letting herself drift. She found that she was listening to the silence. Had not Mother Jean said that in the silence would come the answers to her questions? No answers had come yet, then, she would listen harder.

"The Valley. The Valley," murmured a woman's voice suddenly. It came from one of the back bench sitters, a low breathy sound. Sarah's years of training kept her from looking around to identify the speaker.

"The Valley, the Valley," came a soft answer near her.

"Love in the Valley." It was Ann's tremulous whisper that really got them started. "Love in the Valley."

"Love, love, love," several women called out, their voices almost singing the words. "Love, love, love."

And then the men joined the chorus. "Love, love, love," they boomed. "Love, love, love." One stuttering pace behind came Brother John's reedy echo. "Love."

A single warm, comforting voice rose above them. It was Mother Jean. Someone had once told Sarah that Mother Jean had been a famous singer in the World. It could be so, for her voice always floated effortlessly over them all with the kind of easy authority the Mother of a community should have. *"Mother's* love," her voice cautioned, reminding them of her own feelings for them, recalling them to Mother Ann Lee. "Mother's love," sang the clear, joyful tones.

"Love, love, love," boomed the voices from the men's side. "Love, love, love." They were moving now, swaying on the benches, and the benches' groaning complaint was folded into their song.

"Mother's love," answered the women now, a full chorus.

"Father's love," ventured Father James's nasal voice loudly. It was a reminder of the dual leadership: mother *and* father, the dual incarnation of God — Ann Lee *and* Christ. "Father's love."

Sarah looked over and saw Father James jerk his head up as he spoke. His face looked triumphant as he sang it once again. "Father's love!"

Over Father James's face Sarah suddenly saw another face imposed, a face covered with a dark, curly beard and dark laughing eyes that invited her to laugh, too. His teeth were white and strong, and there was a pronounced gap between the center two. He smiled, and his mouth formed the word, "Daughter."

Sarah stood up, trembling, and raised her hands. "Father," she cried out. Then, as quickly, the laughing man faded, and in his place was the pinched, watchful face of Father James. Sarah covered her mouth and started to sit again, but the other women rose up after her and reached for her, twisting her away from the men's benches in a serpentine movement that turned quickly into a shuffling dance. "Mother's love, mother's love, mother's love," they sang to her, pushing her backward in time to their words. She was forced to go with them, stumbling against the rhythm. She heard the floorboards protest. Someone's arm was around her waist, and when she tried to twist away, the arm pulled tighter and carried her along.

She heard, as if in rough echo, the men's booming voices. First they sang "Father's love," counterparting every verse of the women. Then their thrusting voices began to change, the words began to change, and the rhythm of the snaking dance began to change, too. It became faster, less sure, more pulsing. And at last even Sarah gave way to it, throwing her head back and singing out, calling out, crying out, "Father, mother, love, love, love," until she was no longer sure what she was saying.

The room was spinning with bodies, some leaping, some turning, some clapping their hands. One man jumped up and slapped the ceiling beam with his hands, shouting, "Love lifts me high, high, *high*." Others copied him, though none was able to more than graze the beams with extended fingertips. The leaping man hit the beam once again, crying out in a startling loud tenor, "Higher!"

And then Sister Agatha began to shake and sob. "Mother's love," she cried out. "I need it. I want it. Mother's love. Hold me, Mother Ann. Hold *me*."

Without thinking, Sarah started to move toward Agatha's voice. "I am coming," she called. "I am coming." But someone's hand was at the small of her back, pushing. She felt the quick, sharp jab, looked over her shoulder and saw Ann's face right behind her, flushed and victorious. She slipped, reached out for some support, and, finding none, fell heavily to the floor. The singing and shouting went on. There was a foot on her arm, a knee on her aching right shoulder. "No," she screamed fiercely in pain, in anger, in fear. "No!" She tried to crawl toward the side of the room and could not find a way through the tangle of legs. Her cap had fallen off, hanging around her neck by its strings. Her hair pulled loose of its knot and tumbled down over her forehead and into her eyes. She had started to push the troubling locks aside to see where she could go when a strong hand grabbed her arm and pulled at it. She stumbled to her feet and looked up.

It was the brother from the lawn. He had *touched* her. A man had touched her. She glanced around quickly to see if anyone had noticed, but in the swirling mass of bodies, she could find no staring eyes. She shrank away from him, trembling.

"Do not be afraid," he said, his voice so low she could scarcely distinguish it over the singing shouts of the others.

Sarah took a deep breath and willed herself to be calm. She tucked a curl behind her ear and whispered back in a voice hoarse with shame, "I am not afraid."

He took a step closer to her, and she backed away. It seemed part of the dance.

"You are Abel," she said, thinking suddenly of Sister Ann's list.

He smiled for a moment, and she saw that his teeth were white and strong. "So I am," he replied.

Then the dancers were between them, and they were whirled apart across the miles of crowded room. But their eyes sought one another and held. Sarah could feel the imprint of his hand on her arm.

They sat on their separate benches once more, men on one side of the room, women on the other. The silence barely contained them all. Under the men's shirts perspiration flowed freely. The women patted their temples with handkerdchiefs or dabbed daintily at their upper lips. Brother Frank brought out his pipe, though he did not light it, rubbing the long stem lightly between forefinger and thumb. A heavy musky smell settled over the room.

Mother Jean and Father James smiled contentedly. It had been many weeks, months even, since they had had such a satisfying quick meeting. This one had truly been a Shaker *high*. Any unconfessed wickedness, any springtime carnality would surely have been shaken out of the Believers. They looked at one another across the room. Mother Jean nodded. Father James nodded back and closed his eyes.

🐚 8. Sarah

Sarah could not sleep. Her eyes were closed, but she could not sleep. Her limbs ached and her mind was racing. Around her the room's quiet was punctuated by the night noises of the other girls: Elizabeth's bubbling light snores, Mary's deep, heavy breathing, Ann's occasional sighs. Sarah could not recall having ever really listened to them before, but tonight they contributed to her sleeplessness.

She rubbed her arm lightly where Brother Abel had touched her. She knew it was wrong for a boy to touch a girl, wrong for a girl to even think about a boy. Mother Ann Lee, the great foundress, was quite clear on that. Ann the Word, the Bride of the Lamb, had said that they must all forsake the marriage of the flesh. The only love for Believers was brother and sister love, father and mother love. Sarah knew that, and believed that, having heard it so often in classroom and in Meeting. They even sang of it:

> *Love, love, love,*
> *Oh, what pretty loves,*
> *Father loves us, Mother loves us,*
> *I love you and we love one another,*
> *Oh, what pretty love,*
> *Oh, what good, pure love.*

Pure love. Not carnal love. But never, until today, had she really thought about what Mother Ann meant: the marriage of the flesh. She knew she could not have anything more than pure sisterly love for Brother Abel, yet where he had touched her, his flesh had married hers. That must be why she could still feel his hand on her, could still see the way he smiled, could still hear his voice saying, "Do not be afraid."

She rubbed her arm again.

Slowly she opened her eyes and looked at the ceiling. There were tree shadows dancing there, and all at once she felt like swaying with them. She grew dizzy with longing. Under the covers her feet moved on their own. She grabbed up her bedcovers and threw them back. Then she sat up and thrust her legs over the side of the bed.

The floor was chilly underfoot, but Sarah did not mind. She rose, stretched, and went over to the window. A light breeze was threading its way through the trees. Under the moon's eye, the farm paths stood out starkly. A shadow crossed the moon quickly — a night bird on the prowl. It headed up toward Holy Hill.

Sarah thought again of her stocking and shoes. None of the brethren had mentioned finding them up on the Hill. Surely if they had been discovered, she would have been accused. Somehow her things must be up there still, hidden away. Perhaps Mother Ann Lee had shaken her cloak between the shoes and the brethren, preserving them from a man's sight. That was it. Mother was giving her another chance. She was not meant to be discovered. It was a gift of love.

Sarah made a quick decision: she would go out, now, while the rest of them slept. Go out cloakless and capless and barefoot, with nothing on but her cotton nightshirt, into the cold. Such a chill near-naked pilgrimage would absolve her, dissolve the wedding of her flesh with Abel's. She had not *meant* to be touched by him. It had been Sister Ann's fault, shoving her that way; Sister Ann's sin of being an unforgiving person. That was why Sarah was being given this second chance. She had been punished enough for laughing at Sister Ann, punished enough for violating the Hill, punished enough for leaving her shoes, punished enough for recalling Sister Agatha as her mother. Now she was being given time to repent. And repent she would. She would not even say *his* name again, not even think it. That way, when she returned with her rightful things, she would be one, again, with the other sisters in the purity of their love. She would labor hard to make everything right. Mother Lee had once said that the marriage of flesh was a covenant with death. And was this not a small death she was feeling now, alone and cut off from the sleeping sisters of her family? All she wanted was the love of her sisters and brothers, to be living with them as unsullied as an angel in the paradise of New Vale.

Sarah turned from the window. Tiptoeing past the beds, she made her way out the door and down the creaking stairs.

Only Sister Ann, half-awake, stirred in her bed.

The women's door was locked tight and Sarah could not unbolt it. Hesitantly she crossed the hall to the men's side, wondering briefly if the purity of her pilgrimage would be compromised. To start by sinning — for it was a sin for her to be on that side of the building, the side where the men walked every day, where *he* walked every day.

"I must not think about *him*," she whispered the reminder to herself.

Because she was still young and therefore presumed to be more susceptible to impure thoughts and feelings, she was not allowed to clean the men's side of the Dwelling House or to dust and sweep their sleeping rooms.

She looked around shyly. This was the place where men's fingers had trailed along the banisters, where their hands had touched the latch, where their shoulders had pushed against the door. It seemed unreasonable to her that it should look so much like the women's side.

She touched the door latch and, unaccountably, it moved. The door yielded to the slightest pressure of her shoulder and opened. Surely that was another sign. She held the door tightly so that it would not slam shut behind her and leave her outside in the cold.

For it was cold, colder than she had expected. She shivered but reminded herself that if she could do this one thing, this chilly pilgrimage, then she would be pure again and safe. Safe for all eternity.

"Dear God," she prayed out loud, "dear Mother Ann, protect me." Her voice was thinned out by the wind. Folding her arms across her chest in an effort to stay warm, and setting her teeth together to keep them from chattering, she ran around the side of the building. Her feet crunched on the path. Pebbles bruised her soles. As she passed the corner of the house, a shadow moved out of the bushes. She cried out faintly and almost fell. Someone knew. She was found out. Her sins were too many. Mother Ann had left her. What would happen to her now?

A low voice whispered, "I knew you would come. I knew. I knew." There was laughter in that voice. "I saved your things for you. No one else knows. No one need ever know. Here."

She dared to look up into his face. "Abel," she said at last, giving his name back to him as a gift. "Brother Abel."

He said nothing but handed her the shoes and stockings. They were both careful not to let their fingers touch.

Sarah held the shoes and hose to her breast as if she held precious jewels. "I do not know how to thank you," she whispered, wondering at the same time why she was not more afraid, standing this way, this close to a brother. Alone together. In the dark. *The dark*. That must be the reason. It was as dark as Mother Ann Lee's cloak. They were both wrapped in the cloak, safe from impure thoughts and feelings.

"Just take your things and go, Sister Sara," said Abel. "I need no thanks but your smile."

She smiled shyly and looked down at the ground. Then she turned and ran along the path to the door. At the door she stumbled in her haste and glanced back. He had not followed. For a moment she was strangely disappointed. Then, clutching the shoes and hose even more tightly against her body, she pushed the door open and ran down the hall. She took the stairs two at a time.

When she slipped into her bed and drew the covers up over her head, she breathed, "Thank you, Mother Ann," into the bedclothes. But when she finally fell asleep, it was not Mother Ann Lee who filled her dreams.

April 29, 1854

☙ 9. Abel

For two days Abel puzzled over his feelings, picking through them as carefully as a grader sorting fruit. He had thought that giving back the shoes and hose would end his uneasy union with Sister Sarah. But the relief he *should* have felt had never occurred. Instead, he was left feeling that something was only half-begun: a seed planted but not harvested, a calf conceived but not birthed. The images that stayed with him were all of fruitfulness and bearing.

"Just the spring jimjams," he said out loud as he and Brother Andrew helped Joshua. They were loading a wagon with jars of applesauce, elderberry wine, powdered pumpkin packed in cans for pies, currant wine, rose water, and the famous Shaker herbs; wares prepared for sale to the World's folk, packaged in bright labels that had been printed at the Harvard community. "Just the spring jimjams," Abel repeated. He hoped that one or the other of them would ask him what he meant. Then he would be forced to confess. The weight of his feelings oppressed him. Yet try as he might, Abel could not bring himself to talk openly.

But Brother Andrew apparently did not hear him. And Brother Joshua just nodded at his words as he backed the bay mare into the traces, readying the horse for her part in the journey. Soon Brother Joshua and Brother Jackson would be gone on a week-long selling trip across Massachusetts. They would rest at night with sympathetic Worldly folk. Then after an overnight with the Harvard Shakers, they would return, bringing money from their sales and letters and news of the East Coast brothers and sisters.

Joshua patted the horse several times. Then with a bit of an effort, he hauled himself up onto the seat, taking the reins in hand.

Impulsively Abel put a hand on Joshua's knee. "I wish . . . I wish I could be going out with you," he replied.

"Your time will come," Joshua replied. "When you are more settled."

"But it is because of that, because of the unsettling, I want to go." Abel wanted to say more, but just then Brother Jackson appeared with a long list and a wallet packed with letters.

"Time to be going," Brother Jackson said. He swung himself up onto the seat next to Joshua. " 'Tis a fine, bright spring day for traveling. But as far as we go, I tell you, what I like best is the trip coming home."

Joshua leaned over and spoke so that only Abel could hear him. "Trust yourself, boy." Then he straightened and clicked his tongue. The horse started off, straining at first against the collar, then pulling steadily.

Brother Andrew ran on ahead and opened the gate, waiting there until the cart and horse passed through.

Abel walked thoughtfully to the gate after them. He knew that Brother Joshua trusted him. He wondered if he dared trust himself. Out loud he said, "Someday, someday *I* will go out on such a trip."

Andrew, his eyes crinkling against the bright sun, stared after the wagon. It was almost obscured by dust as it traveled down the road. "It is not something I long for," he said. "I agree with Brother Jackson."

"I do not mean I want to *stay* in the World," said Abel. "I just want to *see* it."

Brother Andrew shook his head. "There is only one end of that road that tempts me."

"Who said anything about temptation?" Abel sounded sharper than he meant.

"Everything is a temptation," replied Andrew calmly. "One must fight against the serpent every day." He pushed the gate, and it closed with a satisfying *snick*.

The boys walked back to the Dwelling House in silence. Andrew had a slight smile on his face, but Abel still could not shake his discontent. He thought about it through lunch and well into the afternoon's work. Helping move a beehive and two swarms of bees from behind the round barn to the meadow near the orchard, he was still puzzling over it. Because he was not paying attention, he was stung painfully several times on his left hand.

"That hand looks bad, Brother Abel," said Brother Frank. "I think a poultice is warranted. Off with you. Jonas and Andrew and I will finish here. But remember, bees need your complete attention. If you do not give it to them voluntarily, they manage to get it in unsubtle ways of their own." He laughed, not maliciously, but in the openhearted way that always guaranteed him an appreciative audience. Jonas and Andrew smiled with him. Even Abel gave a quick chagrined snort, though, in truth, his hand hurt a great deal and was already swelling noticeably.

Walking back to the Dwelling House, Abel held the injured left hand with the right. He tried to concentrate on the pain, letting it flood over him and blot out all other feelings.

Down the path toward him came two of the younger sisters on their way to the Wash House with large baskets of linen. As they came closer, he stepped off the path to let them by. They looked modestly at the baskets they carried. He stared down at his feet, but as they passed he heard the rustling of their skirts. It made a provocative sound that he had never noticed before. Stepping back onto the path, he went on, but a part of him still listened to the receding swishing of the sisters' skirts.

He went into the Dwelling House and up the stairs. There was no one in the Nurse Shop, and he looked in bewilderment at the array of bottles on the shelves. He did not know one remedy from another. In fact he had never been in the Nurse Shop except the one time he had helped bring in Brother Jonas, who had driven a nail through his finger. He would have to find Elder Eben or Father James. They, in turn would seek out Mother Jean and speak to her. She was the one who would probably know the proper ingredients. Of course, by then, he thought, I shall either be cured on my own or my hand will have fallen off from neglect. He looked down at the hand. It seemed less swollen than before, though it was beginning to itch.

He had started to leave the Nurse Shop, convinced he no longer needed help, when two sisters came down the hall. Backing up quickly, he turned sharply and slammed his left hand against the door. It was so painful that he cried out. He heard an answering gasp from one of the sisters. Not daring to look up directly, he still caught a glimpse of one of them with her hand over her mouth. It was Sister Mary, Black Mary, her glasses sliding down her nose. In the children's house she had always been first to sing out at Meeting.

"You will need a poultice for that. A bee sting?" It was the other sister speaking. He knew without looking at her that it was Sara. Sister Sara. He did not dare to show his recognition. Keeping his voice emotionless and low, he answered, "Yes, Sister."

"Sister Sara!" came Mary's quick rebuke. He could see her hand on Sara's sleeve. "Let us find Mother Jean. She will help him."

"We need only get the medicine for him quickly. A sting wants immediate attention. He can apply it himself. That surely cannot be a sin."

"But tarrying here with him . . ." Mary replied uncertainly.

"Then we shall have to be very quick. And not tarry," said Sara.

They moved briskly into the room. He waited by the side of the door, ready to bolt at the first sound of someone on the stairs. He could hear their voices conferring as they read the labels to one another.

"Here is Angelica. That is supposed to be good."

"But it says to first steep in hot water."

"Well, here then is Juice of House Leek. I know *that* is good for an inflammation."

Mary's giggle stopped them both. "He would smell of onions for days. And so would we."

"Here. This is what we want. Elder-Flower Water."

Suddenly a wet cloth smelling of Elder-Flower Water and wonderfully cool was pressed onto his hand. He sighed.

"Sister Mary, I forgot the bottle on the shelf. This cloth should be damper. Could you get it?" Sister Sara asked.

Uncomplaining, Mary went back to the shelves, and Sara whispered to him, "There. That is all I can do. Now we are even."

Abel dared to whisper back, summoning courage from some private corner. "Come out again tonight, Sister Sara. Please. I need to talk to someone, and my confessor, Brother Joshua, has gone into the World selling." Even as he spoke, Abel was amazed at the desperate need in his voice.

"Brother Abel!" came her shocked reply. "There are many brothers to listen to you. Ask one of them."

"They hear but they do not listen," Abel said.

"Here is the bottle." It was Mary. She thrust the bottle into Abel's hand, and the girls went out the door.

He could hear their shoes tip-tapping down the stairs and thought, She did not say yes. But as he went down the men's stairs, the Elder-Flower poultice tied loosely around his hand, he had another thought: But she did not say no.

❧ 10. Sarah

They hear but they do not listen," Sarah murmured to herself as she and Mary went down the stairs. They had been up on the second floor putting away the clean linen.

"What did you say?" asked Mary.

But Sarah did not answer. In one short sentence, seven small words, Brother Abel had summed up her own feelings. For which of her friends, the sisters with whom she shared everything, *really* listened to her needs?

Black Mary at her side, dear, loving Mary who frequently heard voices from the past speaking to her and through her in Meeting and had, even as a child, conversed with General Washington and Jesus, Mohamet and Mother Ann Lee. She would never listen to the kinds of voices that spoke to Sarah up on Holy Hill: the voice of the little peeping smudge bird, the chirping songs of insects, the ghostly braving of the great owl that lived high up in the maple trees.

And Sister Elizabeth, sensible Sister Elizabeth, who was organized and forthright and honest. She had come as a twelve-year-old orphan to New Vale two years ago, with her Shaker virtues already intact. Would she listen to the same things that Sarah wanted her to hear? The sounds of the laughing man in the smoky room? For all her obvious virtues, Sister Elizabeth did not know how to laugh.

And Sister Ann, whey-faced and whiny, but her sister nonetheless. Could she talk to Sister Ann, whose paper visions remained unshared? Could she say, "Sister Ann, I will tell you my dreams if you tell me yours"?

Or Sister Agatha, who had once held her and sung lullabies in a low, comforting voice in the World and who sometimes had opened her arms lovingly in Meeting. Would Sister Agatha tell her what happened to the ragdoll in the cradle, or say the words of the lullaby, or name the laughing man?

Mother Jean said she must trust the silence, but she heard no comfort in it. And Sister Agatha now offered only slaps. And who else among the forty other sisters did she *really* know? She, Sarah, needed to speak and be heard. And so, it seemed, did he. Brother Abel. She understood his need, and she owed him that much, at least. He had saved her when she might have been hurt in Meeting. And he had saved her again when she might have been found out. He was Mother Ann's instrument. She was not sure why.

66

Yes, she thought, she *would* go out one more night, this very night, and find him. And listen. Perhaps when she was through listening to him, he would turn around and do the same for her.

Sarah and Mary continued down the stairs. Mary was humming softly, the hymn about "simple gifts." Sarah smiled. "The gift to listen," she said aloud. But Mary, humming, did not hear.

Night could not come fast enough for Sarah. In her bed, waiting for the others to sleep, she went over her plans. She was both frightened and exhilarated by the thought of meeting Brother Abel. To listen and to be listened to.

She suddenly remembered sitting on her mother's lap and listening to stories and poems with great intensity in the smoky room. Though she had not thought about them in years, Worldly rhymes and tales being forbidden to Shaker children, she thought she might recall a few lines. Closing her eyes, she summoned up one of them, a knee-bouncing game:

> *Trot, trot to Boston.*
> *Trot, trot to Lynn,*
> *Look out, Sarie,*
> *You're going to fall in. . . .*

And the wonderful sensation of falling, falling, falling and being caught up again at the very last possible moment. She shook herself awake. She could not, would not let herself fall asleep. That would be a kind of betrayal.

The settled hush of the room was accentuated by the breathing of the sleeping sisters. Sarah sat up, drew the covers back, and put her feet over the side of the bed. She stood carefully, avoiding the one creaking board that bridged her bed and Mary's. Feeling her way in the dark to the wall, she found her shoes and stockings. She slipped the stockings on, standing awkwardly first on one foot and then the other, but she decided to carry her shoes to avoid extra noise until she was down the stairs. She took her heavy cloak from its peg. It would be cold outside, and how could she *listen* above the chattering of her own teeth?

Tiptoeing from the room, she stood a moment to be sure there were no other sounds. If she was caught now, it would look as if she were meeting Brother Abel for carnal purposes. *Nothing* could be further from their minds, else how could Mother Ann allow it? The Dwelling House was still.

"Mother Ann," Sarah whispered into the dark, "be with me. I must find out if the gift to listen is *my* gift."

Then she went down the stairs.

❧ 11. Abel

They walked side by side without touching toward the barn. They had decided it was the only place where they might stay warm. There was a chill wind blowing. Voices could carry on that wind.

Abel kept glancing over at her as if reassuring himself that she was actually there. The moonlight touched her hair, her cheeks. The wind blew curls across the bridge of her nose. She flicked them away with a quick, graceful gesture.

Abel opened the white gate that stood in the middle of the fence, a gleaming sentinel. Then they walked through and around to the driveway, Abel leading the way. He lifted the iron latch on the big wooden door and pulled it open. The door protested with a loud groan. Abel flinched.

At the door Sara hesitated. Abel thought she was reluctant to enter, that she was loath to be alone with him, shut up inside that great stone hollow. And he could understand that. For a Shaker, to be even this close, alone, without the chaperonage of others, was a sin almost beyond confessing. But when she looked at him questioningly, the moonlight painted her face with a clear light. He realized that she simply did not know the way. She was not old enough to have been one of the spring milkers and had never been inside the barn before.

He walked in first. She followed close behind, as if afraid to lose him in the dark. The scent of her was compounded of night air and barn hay and the musk he had smelled on her stockings. It made his heart race. He breathed deeply and went on. The door groaned shut behind them.

He heard her gasp and turned to answer her unspoken question. "Here," he said. "I am here. Follow the sound of my voice." He knew the barn so well he did not hesitate to find his way through it in the dark, but he walked slowly for Sara. He kept his voice soft but still loud enough to guide her. He led her carefully around several wagons, pointing out a dangerous shaft, an extra wagon wheel, on the floor.

"I did not think we would want to talk down there among the cows and mules and oxen," he said. "I fear their smell might give offense. It is a strong smell, especially if you are not used to it so close."

She laughed, an airy, bubbling sound. "Offend me? Why should it? It is a natural smell," she said. "And standing here, I suddenly remember cows. *And* their smell."

"Remember?" It seemed a peculiar word.

"Yes, remember. When I was of the World — I *was* till I was four, you know — my Worldly father owned a milch cow. And a horse, too, I think. It is most peculiar but I recall it now, all of a sudden. A cow named Marybelle."

"A *human* name?" For a Shaker such a thing was unthinkable.

"Yes, Marybelle. Are not smells a wonderful aid to memory?" She laughed again. This time Abel laughed with her. "I can see pictures in my mind."

Abel closed his own eyes. He tried to find some memories there, but saw only an after-image of the windows in the barn.

"I remember . . . one Christmas Eve he brought me into our barn. Oh, it was not such a grand stone barn as this — more of a shed, really. But it was dark, even darker than this great cavern. My father set the forge fire glowing. I can see that clearly, the puffing bellows blowing up the coals."

"He must have been a blacksmith," Abel volunteered. "We could use one here at New Vale."

"A blacksmith, yes. I remember now. Does memory lean on memory?" she asked. And when Abel had no answer, she continued. "If you had begged me to name my Worldly father's work this morning, I could not have told. But now I remember. Yes, a blacksmith. Oh, Brother Abel, that I could have forgotten so much till now!"

Suddenly he wanted to touch her hand and say how he felt. Or take her hair and thread it between his fingers. He wondered how he could dare to even think up such sins, and he pushed them away from his mind. To forestall such thoughts arising anew, he began to talk to her of the barn. It was a subject far safer than her memories.

"Round barns, they say, keep the devil from hiding in the corners. This one can hold three or four hundred tons of hay. And sometimes, when the new-mown hay is brought into the center mow, the air blowing around it makes so much steam rise you could wash your hands in it." The chattering of his own voice embarrassed him. He wondered if she thought him incredibly stupid. "I . . . I sound as if I were trying to sell you this property," he finished dryly.

He was rewarded with a laugh that ended in a gasp as she stumbled against him.

"Did you hurt yourself?" he asked quickly. He stood still so that she might know where he was and move away.

"No," she said. "But I have just remembered something more. My father, my Worldly father, promised me that the animals would talk to me if I could but stay awake on Christmas Eve to listen. 'Till midnight,' he said. But I fell asleep, and I never heard a word."

"A word," Abel repeated.

"We slept all night in the barn, my father and I. And the next morning, when we went back to the house, the midwife said that . . . that . . ." She hesitated, as if testing the truth of the memory first before offering it to him.

"She said," he prompted gently.

"She said the new baby had died at the birthing. It was the fourth, I think, in five years. Three before me and one after. The others had lived several months before . . . before . . . I knew only the last, poor little thing. Blue colored and wrapped in a scrap of blanket. And then Mother brought me here."

"Mother Ann?"

"No, my Worldly mother." She hesitated a moment as if about to add something. Then she just repeated slowly, "My *Worldly* mother." There was another short silence. Abel did not dare interrupt it. And then suddenly her words tumbled forth. "She said my father was dead as well, though she would not let me see him. Nor stay for the burying. We had to just leave and go. I wanted to kiss him good-bye. Even dead. I could have stood it. She said the Shakers would take us in so long as we had no father. That they would give us a new father. Only Father James wasn't like . . . didn't laugh . . . she said I was to forget who we were and to learn only who we would be. Not mother and daughter but sisters. Not sinners but saints. And I tried. Really tried. Only sometimes lately I seem to remember the wrong things. Like the way he laughed and her arms around me and lullabies and . . ." She began to sob suddenly and without warning.

Abel did not know what to do. He did not understand why she was weeping. He had seen adult sisters and brothers weep in Meeting, but it was joyful, explosive weeping in which they could all join. This was so sad. So solitary. Was she weeping about the dead, blue-colored baby or her father's dying? Was she weeping about the forgetting or the remembering — or something else? He turned around and stood awkwardly, hands at his sides. Several times he tried to say something, but could think of nothing to say. And still her private mourning went on.

At last he put his arms out stiffly and drew her to him. She did not move toward him of her own accord, but she did not move away either. He pushed her head down on his chest. He meant to comfort her like a child, saying, as he had often done with the younger brothers in the children's order, "It is all right. I am here." But when his hand touched her hair, it was thick and springy and seemed to have a life of its own under his fingers. Instead of patting her head and speaking, he simply held her wordlessly. He felt he could go on standing that way for the rest of his life.

But at last she got control of herself. She drew away from him, making a snuffling noise and wiping her nose with the back of her hand. She whispered, "I am sorry. I just remembered I was supposed to be here to listen to you. Forgive me." She gave a small, self-deprecating laugh. Then she found a wagon and scrambled up onto it.

Abel stood apart from her and, with deliberate casualness, leaned against the wagon wheel. He could hear her snuffling still, could see her silhouette outlined against the dusty window glass. He wondered if she could hear the frantic beating of his heart. The sound of it threatened to overwhelm him.

He forced himself to breathe deeply. "At least you had a Worldly mother and father for a time," he said. "They found me on the Meeting House doorstep in a willow basket. I was wrapped in a piece of horse blanket. There was a note pinned to it that said 'Keepe him till he be Abel.' That is how I was named."

"My name is Sarah," she said softly.

He was surprised and his voice showed it. "I know that."

"With an *h*." She said it fiercely, as if daring him to argue.

He thought a minute. "With an *h*. It is prettier that way."

"Yes!" she breathed. "Yes."

"I will remember," he promised. "Sarah. With an *h*."

74

She was utterly quiet for a moment. At last she took a deep, audible breath. "Dear Brother Abel, who has had no mother. *I* will be your mother. And I will listen when your confessor is not here. And . . . and when he *is* here, too, if that is what you desire."

It was Abel's turn for silence. He could hear an ox moving heavily below them. A board creaked underfoot. Then suddenly a bird flew through the loft. It so startled them that they both began talking at once to cover their fear.

"I do not need a . . ." Abel began, his voice rougher than he meant.

"My mother . . ." Sarah, started, her voice unusually high.

They laughed uncertainly, and Sarah shifted a bit on the wagon as if trying to find a comfortable position.

"You speak first," she said.

"No, you," Abel answered.

"We must be honest with one another," she said. "Honest and clear. Good listening needs that. Always."

"Always," Abel said quickly, hearing the promise in her words. He put his hand over his heart.

"Then what were you saying?"

Abel felt his face begin to burn again. "I said . . . I said . . . that I do not need . . . do not need . . ." He could not go on.

"A mother!" Sarah finished for him. "But of course you do. We *all* do. That is what Mother Ann Lee taught. That is why the leader in the female line is called Mother. And the leader in the male line Father. But *you* need something more. A listener. So

I will be your listener and your sister *and* your mother."

"And my friend," Abel said in a sudden whisper, surprising himself.

Sarah was silent, so silent that Abel was afraid he had lost her. Oh, he could see that her body was still there. But the rest of her had suddenly gone, and the silence stretched between them so taut that he feared it would break.

Then with a sigh Sarah answered him. "I do not know what you mean, Brother Abel. A friend? With a man? I only know about sisters. And mothers."

"I do not know either," he said, moving closer to her in the dark. He could hear her move a little away from him. "I only know that I want us to discover it together."

He heard the quick intake of her breath. "I am afraid. Oh, Brother Abel, I am so afraid. How may we remain angels if we become friends? Men and women may not . . . may not . . . the marriage of the flesh is a burning in hell. Once I was burned, helping Sister Agatha in the kitchen. It was only a small burn. On my hand. This hand." She held up her hand, and he could see its shadowy form. "But I can still recall its feel."

He answered slowly, "Is the opposite of an angel a devil?" When she did not answer, he answered himself. "I think that the opposite of an angel may be a simple everyday human being. Someone of the World."

"Of the World," she echoed.

"Like your mother and father," Abel said.

"And like yours, whoever they are."

"And like mine," he agreed finally.

76

Her voice was almost as insubstantial as a breeze blowing over him. "It will have to be a secret, Brother Abel."

"It will be."

"I like secrets," she mused. Her voice was suddenly as light as a child's. Then it changed. "I know they are wrong — secrets. I know that surely." She made a small, wry laughing sound. "My shoulders still ache from my last secret, and I am very much afraid."

He did not understand what she meant, but it did not matter. He knew the proper answer and gave it. "Then I shall have to have the courage for both of us," he said, speaking more bravely than he felt. "Surely *my* shoulders are strong enough for two."

Her sigh touched him. "Thank you. Oh, *friend* Abel, I do, do thank you." He could hear her joy bubbling up and catching in her voice. Then she looked upward. "And I thank you, too, Mother Ann."

Abel closed his eyes and listened as she sat back in the wagon. The silence between them was rich and full of meaning. He did not feel any need to puncture it with words.

After many minutes he heard her sigh again and shift her weight. Then came the satisfying tap of first one shoe, then the other onto the barn floor. He opened his eyes.

She was standing. "Come, my brother, my child, my friend. We had better go back to the Dwelling House before we are missed." Her voice was so calm, so soothing that Abel began to wonder which of them really had the courage.

"But will I see you again?" He asked it knowing that he feared her answer.

She laughed. "We have seen each other every day of our lives in New Vale. I expect we will continue."

"Seen — and yet not seen," he said.

"They hear but they do not listen," she answered.

"Yes. Never like this."

She agreed. "Never, never like this." She paused a moment. "Tomorrow night?"

"Tomorrow night," he echoed. "Do you solemnly swear it?"

"I swear it, my only friend."

He moved toward her quickly and put out his hand, but she walked around the wagon and found the door without him. She was one step before him all the way back to the Dwelling House. Her steps were so long he almost had to break into a trot to keep up. She slipped through the men's door well ahead of him.

By the time he followed, she was a shadow, a mist, a wisp of fog that crossed to the women's stairs and was gone. He did not even have time to whisper good night. But the scent of her stayed with him as he slowly tiptoed up to his room.

April 30, 1854

❧ 12. Sarah

It seemed to Sarah that she had barely fallen asleep when she woke to the challenge of the morning bell. The sunlight lay draped across the foot of her bed, lending a festive air to the blanket. She moaned as she tried to rise, for she could feel every muscle arguing against it. She was as tired as if she had not slept all night.

Last night! Guiltily she glanced toward the wall where her everyday shoes stood innocently side by side with her Sabbath shoes. She wondered briefly if it had all been a fancy, like one of Sister Ann's grubby little paper dreams. But her shoulder hurt too much, and when she looked more closely at the shoes, she noticed a single piece of hay caught under one heel, its golden shaft pointing accusingly at her. Sarah prayed that no one else would notice, but in her secret heart she doubted anyone would. So much of what she had done the last few days and nights had passed unnoticed that she was totally convinced Mother Ann Lee was protecting her.

She sat up in bed and swung her legs over the side. As her feet touched the smooth wood floor, she remembered the barn floor, full of uneven places. Then suddenly Brother Abel's face rose before her. His broad open forehead with the dark bangs cut straight across. The strong arched nose. The curve of his mouth with the thin upper lip. The chin with its sharp cleft. What a good friend she had in him. She remembered him saying, "Sarah. With an *h*," in his slow, considering way. She smiled and closed her eyes.

"Shame," came a hissed warning.

Sarah opened her eyes quickly and saw that the other girls were already up and dressed. Mary was finishing pulling her black curly hair back into its knot, and Elizabeth was drying her face. It was Ann, standing at the foot of Sarah's bed, hands on hips, who had spoken.

"Shame," she said again, her pinched white face flushing. "Sluggard. We lack but five minutes till cleaning. And you are still abed. And smiling about it as well."

Quietly improvising, Sarah answered, "I had a gift. A gift that Mother Ann . . . shook her cloak over me." It was not exactly untrue, she thought. Besides, was truth something that could be measured: four parts out of five being truthful means a statement is true? Only eight parts out of seventeen, and the statement is a lie? Surely God and Mother did not count like that.

80

At Sarah's words, Mary came over, tying her cap strings. "What did Mother do?"

Suddenly ashamed at her deception, for Mary was such a loving, open soul, Sarah could do nothing but continue inventing. "Her cloak. She shook it between me and . . . Satan. And then it covered me and kept me warm. And I knew no harm could befall me. Like this." She made a movement as if taking a cloak from its wall peg, then swung the imaginary cloak up and around her shoulders. "And I was warm, warm, warm," she began to sing.

The other girls joined in involuntarily. "Warm, warm, warm," they sang back.

"And safe, safe, safe," Sarah added on three higher notes.

"Safe, safe, safe," sang Mary and Elizabeth.

"Safe from what, I wonder," Ann said sourly.

Elizabeth was properly scandalized. "It was a *gift*," she said in her tiny, high-pitched voice.

"From Mother Ann," added Mary, putting on her glasses.

"Not all gifts come from Mother," said Ann stubbornly. "And I do not see why Mother should vouchsafe a gift to a sluggard. A sluggard and a . . . a sneak." She put her hands together over her stomach righteously, right hand on top, and left the room. In the silence that followed, Sarah could feel her heart pounding madly.

"What does she mean — a sneak?" asked Mary at last. She turned to Sarah, sliding her glasses back up the bridge of her nose. "Do you know what she means?"

"It was a gift," said Elizabeth again, quieter, less certain.

"Never mind," said Sarah. "Perhaps Sister Ann is right. Perhaps it was not a gift. Perhaps it was occasioned by last night's supper."

Mary cocked her head to one side. "But last night was stew and mealy potatoes. With dried apple pie for dessert. Your favorite."

"So it was. I probably ate too much," agreed Sarah cheerfully, getting dressed as quickly as she could. She bent over her shoes and picked off the piece of hay, careful to keep her back between the offending shoe and the other girls. She hid the piece of hay under her pillow as she straightened her bed. But she could not help adding over her shoulder, "Mother's cloak was *very* warm."

When she stood up again, she was smiling slightly. "Sister Ann is right about one thing. I *have* been a slugabed today. But now I am ready — and in plenty of time to do my share of our work." She smoothed her skirt as she spoke.

It was Sarah and Mary's turn to clean their room; Ann and Elizabeth were to work in the hall. So Elizabeth left without another word.

Mary hung the chairs up on their pegs and began sweeping while Sarah made up the beds. They knew the routine so well that they did not have to speak about it. They dusted and swept in companionable silence, though the lines of the Sweeping Gift, which they used twice a year for housecleaning the entire community, ran around and around in Sarah's head. "Sweep, sweep and cleanse your floors," sang her mind. Everything this morning seemed to have a sprightly tune accompanying it.

She knew that, as she worked, some of the older women would be cleaning the men's rooms. She wished she could be with them, sweeping Brother Abel's room, making up his bed. He would not be there, of course. The men had to be out of their rooms within fifteen minutes of the rising bell and carrying their own chamber pots so the women could enter five minutes later and clean. She wondered what Abel's room looked like. Was his bedstead painted the same lovely green as hers? Or was it plain? Would his quilt be the same pattern of blue-and-white? Would he have curtains on his windows, with the morning sun streaking patterns on the floor? She had been in the men's rooms only on Union Meeting nights, and though they were similar, they each had small variations. She wondered which one was his. And at night, lying straight in his bed as was commanded, did he make soft whuffling sounds like Elizabeth, whimpers and sighs like Ann, or deeper, rougher snores like Mary? Or did he just lie silent and still till dawn?

Sarah smiled fondly at her questions. She knew they were silly, unshakerly questions, but that did not stop them from tumbling through her head. She went over to the windows and opened each one a few inches, setting the thumbscrews so that the spring air would fill the room all day.

"It is quite warm enough now to air things out," she said. "I should think it will soon be time to take the windows out and wash them." She ran a finger over a corner pane and made a face at the mark she left there.

But Mary did not seem to be paying any attention to Sarah's words. Instead, she asked, "Was Mother's cloak very warm indeed?"

For a moment Sarah hesitated. Surely she could

tell Sister Mary the truth of it, about the cloak and the shoes and Brother Abel and all the rest. Good, solid, loving Sister Mary, whose Worldly parents had both been runaway slaves too poor to bring anything of worth into New Vale but themselves and Sister Mary. They had been too sick to last but one New England winter. Surely Sister Mary would understand. "About Mother's cloak," Sarah began.

"Soft and warm?" Mary whispered.

Sarah bit her lip. Whatever happened, wherever her friendship with Brother Abel led her, she could not drag Sister Mary along. It was her own secret — and Brother Abel's. "Very soft," she said. "And very warm."

"I knew it," Mary said, smiling. "That is how it would have to be."

They went out of the room together, and the spring air finished the cleaning for them.

❧ 13. Abel

Abel slumped at the table. He toyed with his food. Even the cheese, the first of the spring made with new milk, failed to hold his interest. He was tired but, more than that, he had failed to catch Sarah's eye as they came into the dining hall.

She had been looking down at her hands the whole time, ignoring him. And now he had to sit with his back to her. He was sorely tempted to turn around and speak to her out loud. "Friend Sarah," he would say, "have you forgotten your promise?" But of course, he did not.

Brother Andrew elbowed him in the ribs as a reminder, and Abel sat up straighter. He looked with dismay at his plate. It was piled high with food that he did not remember taking and that he certainly had no stomach for eating. Somehow, though, he would have to finish it all. Wasting food was a sin. He pushed a forkful into his mouth mechanically, scarcely swallowing. He followed it quickly with another. His throat began to spasm. He choked and coughed back eggs and mucus onto his plate. His eyes watered. He could not see.

"Brother Abel!" came the nasal voice of Father James across the silence of the room.

Abel hung his head and tried to swallow. His throat hurt terribly.

"I would speak with you after the meal. But so that you do not continue to disturb the others, you may leave. Now."

Abel stood up. He was aware that everyone in the room must be looking at him. He dared a quick glance over his shoulder at the women's side of the room. They were all staring at him openly except for Sarah, who was concentrating on her plate. The only signs that she knew what was happening were the two bright red splotches on her cheeks. He had made a fool of himself in front of her.

Head high, jaw set, Abel walked out of the room. He marched down the hall, and into the Elders' Waiting Room. Once there, he could feel the cold sweat under his arms and a flush on his own cheeks. He could not decide whether he should sit or stand, though he feared that if he did not sit soon, he would fall down. He perched for a moment on one of the wooden chairs set out for visitors. When he felt he had control again, he stood. But once up, he could not be still, shifting from one foot to another unhappily.

The sounds from the dining hall traveled down the corridor to him: the occasional clankings as silverware scraped on a plate, the footsteps of the kitchen sisters. Abel could not understand why those sounds, which had always comforted him before, especially on the early winter mornings when the family ate before sunrise, should suddenly seem so cold and distant. He tried to sing to himself, to borrow courage from a song. The one that came immediately to mind went:

> *I want, I want more love,*
> *Mother's love I want,*
> *I want Mother's love . . .*

But he could not go on with it. He realized with a sudden clear revelation that it was a lie. It was Sarah's love he wanted. Sarah. With an *h*. He had not willed it to be so. He knew that what he desired was the greatest of sins. And he vowed he would do nothing to shame Sarah, to make her sin. The sin, the fleshly love, was all his. He would say nothing to her. But he could not stop himself from feeling what he felt. He sighed her name out loud.

"Sarah."

It seemed to fill up all the corners of the room.

He heard the scrape of benches and, after, the tap-tapping of feet coming down the hall. Abel waited, standing very straight and still. He folded his hands before him, Shaker style, and tried not to fidget.

Father James came into the room and walked over to the writing desk. He pulled out the chair from its place under the desk and sat down. For a long moment he said nothing. He simply looked at Abel disapprovingly, his thin lips drawn together. His hands were clasped in his lap, but the two thumbs kept hitting against one another with a steady beat. Abel tried to look back but could not bear to stare into Father James's eyes. Instead, he looked about three inches over Father James's head and swallowed hard.

At last Father James breathed deeply and folded his thumbs right over left. He made a sound between his teeth that was somewhere between a sigh and a hiss. "Now, Brother Abel, you need not fear to unfold anything to me. I have been very aware of your wanderinng mind. Tell me what troubles you, and together we will labor to set things right."

The words were perfectly ordinary ones. Taken one by one they showed a fatherly concern. But Abel felt they contained some hint of menace, some unspoken threat. That was always Father James's way. Abel wondered if it was Father James's high, whiny voice or his close-set, ferrety eyes that made him *seem* untrustworthy. Yet how could Father James be Father to all of New Vale and not be trustworthy? Abel was the untrustworthy one who had sinned, was sinning still. It was a puzzle for sure. But Abel knew that if he unfolded anything, it would be to Brother Joshua and not to Father James.

"I have nothing to say, Father," Abel began.

Father James sucked air through his teeth. "Nothing? You call that display at the table nothing?"

"I fear I ate too quickly, Father," Abel answered. He looked at the floor.

" '*I fear I ate too quickly*'?" The nasal imitation added self-pity to Abel's words which he knew had not been there before. Involuntarily he shuddered.

"You shake, Brother Abel. Well you might shake, in the fear of the Lord. For the Lord knows that when one of His children has trouble eating, when one of His children is late for meals, when one of His children wanders the hallways at night . . ." He stopped and added, "A father knows these things, too."

Abel looked up abruptly.

"Did you forget that I have ears? Even in sleep I hear my children. I was right, then — it *was* you."

"I do not know what you mean, Father." Abel felt his face close down. "Perhaps there has been someone walking in the halls at night, but I know nothing of it." He said it calmly, hating the deception, hating himself for deceiving, and hating Father James most of all, for making him lie. But if he could keep Sarah from being hurt, he would lie and lie again.

Father James stood and turned his back on Abel,

walking over to the window. He raised his hands palms up and then palms down, as if warming them in the light of the rising sun. "If I am in error about you, Brother, then I ask your forgiveness. But if I am not —" He stopped. Then, as if changing reins, he said, "I would have you concentrate your mind today, as you labor, on Mother Ann Lee's precious words: *Hands to work, hearts to God.*"

It was a dismissal. Abel mumbled his thanks and left. He had morning chores to do. In the barn.

He went into the barn, not by the usual ground floor door but by retracing his steps of the night before. Slowly he walked up the driveway ramp. It was a wonder to him that the barn still looked the same: solid, workaday. Its blocks of gray stone and white mortar were unchanged by Sarah's midnight presence. He lifted the iron latch and hesitated as she had, remembering.

Once inside, he wandered in among the wagons. He could not tell which one she had been sitting on. There was no telltale glow, no special sign. It seemed impossible that only he — and not the barn — had been so changed by a single night.

Nodding at Brother Frank, who was working on a wagon wheel, Abel walked to the railing and stared out over the ground floor. Andrew and Jacob were tossing hay from the center mow over to the cows. The two pair of oxen waited their turns with patient grunts.

"You all right, boy?" came a voice next to him.

"What?" Abel looked up. Brother Frank was by his side.

"Father James straightened everything out with you?" Brother Frank asked. "He always does, you know. If I have a confession, I go to him. He gets to the heart of things, does Father James. Even when we were boys together in the children's order, he would find the heart. I always knew he would be Father someday. He told me so, and I believed him. Now me, I go around and about. Like an old meandering river, no help to anyone. But Father James, he is straight and true as a plumb line. Like an arrow. God's arrow."

An arrow, Abel thought. Straight to the heart. The intent might be to give eternal life, but the result had been a kind of death. "Yes," he said, giving Brother Frank the answer expected. "I know my mind now." Abel nodded. "Thank you, Brother."

"Are you to help me up here, then?"

Abel looked down once more into the bowels of the busy barn. Brothers Andrew and Jacob were no longer in sight. They were probably helping with the milking. "No, I am to help with the cows first and then do Brother Joshua's chores."

"Then what are you doing up here, boy? Get along with you." He slapped Abel on the shoulder. "Perhaps you need to have another little talk with Father James. You are still a bit muzzy, if you ask me. Spring can do that to a man. It is all this fresh earth smell, cows birthing, and the planting, I think."

Abel went down the stairs to the ground floor as quickly as he could, gratefully seeking out the cows, whose questions were easy and whose answers all began with hay.

14. Sarah

No one spoke after Brother Abel had left the dining hall, but Sarah was sure that everyone was staring at her. Her cheeks burned. Her eyes seemed unable to focus. Every bite was dust in her mouth. She Shakered her plate till she feared she would scrape off the design, a simple rendering of the words "New Vale." She placed her knife and fork in perfect position on the plate as slowly as she dared. Anything to prolong the breakfast and to keep Father James from leaving the room.

She was sure that Brother Abel would confess nothing to Father James. She trusted him to be strong. But Father had a strange power, a gift of persuasion. He had always frightened her, though she had never talked to him directly.

But at last the meal was done. There was no more delaying. The Believers stood up, the men leaving the dining hall first. When the women followed, Sarah was in step with the rest.

Her morning duties took her to the Dyeing and Weaving Shop, where she worked alongside Sisters Ruth, Martha, and Faith. It was a duty she usually enjoyed. Faith had a great gift for the loom. Her cloth was always straight and tightly woven. And Sister Martha's color sense was the best in New Vale. The two of them spent almost all their time weaving and dyeing cloth for the Believers' own clothes as well as for the more colorful Shaker cloaks made especially to sell to the World. The cloaks were so popular they brought in a great deal of money for the community. Next to the sale of seeds and herb teas, the cloaks kept New Vale's coffers full.

Sisters Martha and Faith would often lead their helpers in song after song praising work. The room always echoed with their good cheer. But today each trip of the shuttle across the loom sounded like a step down the long hall toward the Elders' Waiting Room. All Sarah could think about was Brother Abel. She waited, unable to sing with the sisters, unable even to talk with them. She waited for a summons. The bright spring day seemed doom-laden.

But as the morning progressed and no summons came, Sarah could feel herself relax. The tightness between her shoulders dissolved. She began to nod to the rhythm of the songs. It really must be true that Mother Ann Lee had placed a cloak on her shoulders. Perhaps that was what a gift was — not an invention but an inspired guess. Brother Abel, Friend Abel must have stood firm, even in the face of Father James's gifted tongue. She should never have doubted him. Doubt, after all, was not a Shaker virtue. She began to hum her own little tune, then was quickly caught up in the song the others were singing, the one Mary had been humming on the stairs.

> " 'Tis the gift to be simple,
> 'Tis the gift to be free,
> 'Tis the gift to come down
> Where we ought to be,
> And when we find ourselves
> In the place just right,
> 'Twill be in the valley
> Of love and delight."

The *click-clack* of the loom counted out the rhythm of the song. Sarah began to dance across the room. First she tried a kind of eager variation of the Square Order Shuffle, then added steps of her own. She felt free of guilt, free of fear. " 'Tis the gift to be simple," she sang happily. " 'Tis the gift to be free."

She skipped from the dye pots to the skeins hanging on hooks on the wall, then to the rows of jars containing the dried roots and herbs used in dyeing: chestnut bark and madder, butternut and flowering hardhack. She brought each one at Sister Martha's command.

Sitting straight-backed at her loom, Sister Faith smiled over at the dancing girl and remarked, "You are a rainbow today. A rainbow after the downpours of the last few days. I wish I still had a ray of that youthful sunshine blessing me." She put a hand to her side and sighed for a moment, stretching.

Sarah stopped abruptly, her skirts still whirling about her. "Downpours? What do you mean, Sister? It has not rained for days."

Sister Ruth laughed. "Dear Sara," she said. "Have you no ear for colorful talk? Do not act slow. It does not become you. Modesty is a virtue, as is simplicity. But slowness is not."

Sarah looked more confused, and Sister Ruth added, "After all, we *all* know what happened."

Sarah felt her heart stop. One minute it was beating and the next it stopped, stuttered, then began to beat loudly again. She turned slowly toward Sister Ruth, who was bent over a vat of red madder dye. "Know? What do you know?" she dared at last. "What *could* you know?"

Faith shook her head and stopped the loom. "Child, child, we know everything. How could such a small community as ours not know everything? Besides, in all faith, how could we miss it? You screamed loud enough for a whole army. And I took two blows on the arm myself. There are bruises I could show you. That Agatha! I do not understand why they let her stay. She is obviously deranged. Now if I were an elder . . ."

"Which you are not," reminded Sister Martha.

"But *if* I were," Sister Faith persisted, "I would send her away." She finished righteously and started up the loom again.

"Away?" Sarah turned back slowly and stared at Faith. She could scarcely breathe. "But why?"

From the dye sink Martha answered her in a low, slow voice. "We knew a woman like her in Salem when we lived in the World, Faith and I. Mad as a hatter she was. She fair killed her own child, who was scarce two years old. She beat the child when her man left. Faith sometimes dreams about it."

"Hush," said Ruth. "Remember who Agatha is . . ." She hesitated with her finger to her lips and nodded toward Sarah.

94

"Of course I remember," said Martha. "But not is. *Was*. And what she *was* in the World to this dear child is no concern of ours here. Here she is Sara's sister as she is ours. As Mother Jean is mother to us all. And I am surprised at *you*, Sister Ruth, reminding us of the World."

Sister Ruth looked properly chastised. "You are right. I just thought . . . but I do agree. She should be sent away. Before she does someone a *real* hurt. Why, I could tell you things she does in our room, things she does to herself when she thinks I do not notice. Why, I have told Mother a hundred times . . ."

"A *real* hurt?" Faith interrupted. "That was real enough for me." She rubbed her arm without missing a beat of the loom.

"Not away," Sarah whispered again, her voice an agony. She remembered suddenly a line from the dream woman's lullaby: "I will guard thee, I will guide thee."

"There, you see, she has a true gift of forgiveness, this child," said Faith, nodding at Sarah. "Mother's precious one. A real gift."

"Come, girl, stop mooning about what cannot be changed. Take these skeins quickly," called out Martha, pulling the freshly dyed wool from the vat with a stick. "But if you drop them, *I* will not be so quick to forgive. 'Tis not my gift, after all."

Sarah took the sticks to the drying hooks, heedless of the red stains on her hands. She turned and spoke to Sister Faith. "They would not *really* send her away, would they? I do not think she meant to harm me, not in her heart. She can be so calm and loving. Sometimes."

"Soonest ended, soonest mended, I say," Sister

Martha called from the sink. "But then, I am not the forgiving sort."

"You already mentioned that, Sister. With you forgiveness takes years," Sister Faith said over the noise of the loom.

"I mean it," Martha continued. "If *Sister* Agatha raises a hand to me, spoon or no spoon, she will find that out. She has gotten away with a great deal these ten years, if you ask me. With her fainting fits and her fasting and the way she has abused this child, singling her out. Do not think it has not been noticed."

Sister Ruth added eagerly, "She sticks pins in her fingers at retiring time sometimes to draw blood. I have seen."

"Thinks she is holy, does she?" Martha snorted, and in a low, breathy imitation of Sister Agatha's voice, she said, " 'My name was Agatha Lanyard, the same initials as Ann Lee.' " She snorted again.

Faith cautioned, "She *is* a hard worker. And, as Sara says, often calm."

Martha went on as if she had not heard. "The same initials! As if that were any excuse for her excesses. If you ask me, she has a gift of madness — and that is all." Martha ended her statement with a final snort.

"Oh, Marfie, you forget yourself," warned Sister Faith, laughing.

"I always do," Martha replied. But she laughed back at Faith comfortably.

The bell cut them short. They tidied up after themselves with spirited efficiency, washed their hands briskly with yellow soap, and went in to dinner.

* * *

The conversation of the sisters and the words "sent away" continued to echo in Sarah's mind. If Sister Agatha was sent away, it would be Sarah's fault; if mad, she had certainly been driven to it by Sarah, by her secrets and her wicked, willful disobedience. Perhaps, Sarah thought, perhaps I *am* an imp of Satan. Perhaps the laughing man was the devil. Except that the face she had seen over Father James's had been the homely face of a rugged man who had laugh lines into the corners of his eyes. Did the devil laugh? Still, her night's activities proved she was a near relation to Satan. Such a thing could not, must not happen again. How could she ever, ever forgive herself if she was the cause of Sister Agatha's being sent away? What would poor Sister do? Where could she go? Sister Agatha was the good Shaker, the honest Shaker, who was trying, still, in her own way to guard and guide Sarah. She, on the other hand, was the wicked one, driven by a soft love she had not even admitted, excusing her actions by saying she was only a listener, a friend. Friend! As if a man and a woman could ever be friends. If anyone should be sent away, Sarah thought, it should be *me*.

As they filed into the waiting room for broad grace time, Sarah saw that Sister Agatha was already sitting with the other kitchen sisters. Her chapped and reddened hands, with bruise marks about the knuckles, lay passively on her lap. Her eyes were closed. In repose her face was lovely, marred only by a deep crease that sat over her eyebrows, the legacy of a lifetime of disappointments.

Without thinking, Sarah broke from the line and

ran over to her. She knelt down, heedless of the startled looks from the others, and began to speak. Her words tumbled over one another in her eagerness to get it all said.

"Sister, forgive me. If I am indeed an imp of Satan, a child of the devil, I repent of it. If I have been wicked, I will be so no more. Please, please, Sister, I *will* be good with you to guard me and guide me. Do you remember the song? I promise. Here is my hand on it." She held out her hand.

Sister Agatha did not move except to open her eyes. As she stared at Sarah, the pale washed-out blue of her eyes seemed to grow pinpoints of orange near the center. She opened her mouth but said nothing.

Sarah bit her lip. "If you will not take my hand, dear Sister Agatha, I will take yours." She grabbed up one of the woman's hands and held it, knuckle against her cheek. "For you are my own dear sister. I know it now. And I am yours."

Sister Agatha pulled her hand away savagely and slapped Sarah across the face, first one cheek, then the other. The sounds were as sharp and as final as gunshots.

"You are none of mine," she cried out in a high, strained voice. "Nor ever were. I reject you. I renounce you. Get behind me, Satan." She leaped up, pushing Sarah over, and ran back into the kitchen.

The silence that greeted her leaving was one of shock. For a long moment no one moved.

At last Sarah pulled herself up and sat down in Sister Agatha's place. She closed her eyes and folded her hands. Only the flushed fingerprints on her cheeks proved the violence that had occurred. Sarah fought successfully against the tears, but she could not help wondering how God's hand could possibly be any harder than Sister Agatha's or His heart colder and more unforgiving.

☙ 15. Abel

Abel sat as straight as possible in the splint-bottomed chair. He tried, as he had tried all day, to fill his mind with lists. In that way he would think about nothing. Mentally, he catalogued the room, Brother Joshua's and Frank's retiring room: two beds, a single dresser, candlestand and stove, a well-polished plank table piled high with hymn books. But the list went too swiftly, and he was left with thinking time. So he began to catalogue the Believers who sat as straight as he did at Union Meeting.

Next to him, on his left, was Brother Andrew, smiling. Brother Andrew had whispered to him, before they had entered, that while the dancing, singing, laboring meetings brought him closer to God, Union Meeting brought him closer to the brethren and sisters of New Vale. Brother Frank, his hands clasped, sat on Abel's right. And on Brother Frank's right, ranged in a stiff row, were Brothers Theodore, Stephen, and Matthew. They were all hardworking and soft-spoken. Though he had known them all his life, Abel found them almost indistinguishable. (Although once, he reminded himself, Brother Theodore had given him a taste of the famous Shaker cider. When he had choked on it, Theodore had laughed and said he would grow to like it. He never had.) They all sat, as was required, with their feet flat on the floor, their backs stiff as boards.

Across the room were seven sisters. None of them was closer than the requisite five feet. Sister Martha, the oldest, had claimed the rocker. Then there was Black Mary. Next to Mary, in a line, were five other sisters whose names he supposed he knew but could suddenly not remember. And what did their names matter to him, anyway? The one he had hoped might be there was not. Sarah. With an *h*.

Union Meeting groups were changed every month so that the brothers and sisters did not become too familiar with one another or form unseemly attachments. Abel had hoped . . . but it was not to be. She was in another room. With another group. He envied the ones in her presence.

They talked, as was demanded, about nothing important. Abel tried to follow the conversations. For a while he maintained a semblance of interest. Brother Frank, who had some commerce with the World's folk selling New Vale handwork, remarked on the terrible plight of the black slaves and what he called "the coming conflagration."

Sister Martha interrupted. "Dear Brother Frank," she said, "perhaps you are too much of the World. It flavors your conversations with a hot spice. You tell us things we need not know. Remember, we are a plain folk. We abjure war. If the World's folk go about enslaving one another and killing one another, it is not for us to ponder."

Frank looked down at the floor during Sister Martha's mildly spoken rebuke. When she was finished, he took his pipe from the table where it had been hidden behind the hymn books. He lit it, and the sound of its drawing filled the room.

"I remember," said Sister Mary suddenly, "being with all the others. In the hot rows. And the white bursts of cotton." She paused. "And the whips."

Sister Martha shook her head, rocking slowly. "You would do better not to remember, my dear little sister. Memory is a treacherous path which some would do well not to tread. If forgiveness is hard, do not make it harder by remembering past sins. You see, I speak to my own weaknesses as well as yours."

Sister Mary was silent and hung her head for a moment. But when she looked up, her smile was radiant. "Mother's cloak is very warm," she said.

That brought a round of nods from everyone. Even Abel was forced to smile.

"I have heard about a new saw that a brother in South Union made with the plans he saw in a dream one stormy March night," Brother Theodore began.

"Ahh," sighed Sister Martha approvingly. "Now *that* is proper Union fare. Tell us more." Her rocker creaked its approval as well.

Brother Theodore went on. Abel, always fascinated by the many Shaker inventions, listened almost eagerly. But Brother Theodore's story was soon over. He knew little about the workings of the saw. He had only heard about it from someone who had had a letter from another brother in South Union, a third-hand delivery.

As Brother Theodore trailed off, one of the older sisters began reminiscing over springs past and telling of her hopes for the new herb gardens. Abel lost the thread quickly, and he started thinking again of Sarah.

He wondered if he had made a complete fool of himself at breakfast. The other Believers did not matter, but what if *she* had thought him a fool, a child, being sent away from the table like that? Such a thing had not happened to him since he had been in the children's order. That was a mile and a million years down the road. He remembered it vividly. It had been a hot summer day. He had made many trips to the water bucket during their garden working time. They had been marched straight from the garden to the pump for a brisk washing. Then without another stop they had gone in for broad grace time. At the dinner table he had suddenly not been able to hold his water. Nor was he allowed to get up, even though he was one of the youngest there. It had been a disaster. The boy's caretaker, an old brother named Jephthah, had seen the puddle steaming under the table. Angrily he had sent Abel from the room. The other boys, especially three newly adopted blood brothers, had teased him for months. They had called him little Brother Unable. Brother Jephthah had been incapable of controlling them. Even the Elders' cautions had not kept the three from their behind-the-hand whisperings. Peculiarly, Abel could not recall any of their names, though their faces suddenly burned vividly in his memory: redheaded, freckle-faced. They had been reclaimed within the year by relatives. When they left, the teasing had stopped. Brother Jephthah had been replaced by Brother Joshua. Abel doubted that Andrew or Jacob or John, who had been with him from the beginning in the children's order, even remembered the incident. Certainly none of them had ever mentioned it to him. He shook his head. How could something that meant *so* much to one mean so little to others? It was a puzzle. Perhaps Sister Martha was right — about memory being a treacherous path.

"You do not agree, Brother Abel?" asked Brother Frank. As the senior brother, he had, along with Sister Martha, the task of trying to guide them all toward union, though sometimes he forgot himself.

"Forgive me, Brother Frank," Abel said quickly. "And forgive me, Sister. Your memories stirred my own. I was remembering something myself."

"Perhaps you would share that memory with us," said Sister Martha, rocking in rhythm to her words. "If it is so powerful as to drown out Sister Charity's lovely past springs and her hopes for the herb gardens, we should certainly like to partake of it." She smiled at him to ease the sting of her rebuke.

Abel looked down at his hands and carefully re-crossed his thumbs, left over right. It was a small insurrection. Mindful of every word, he said, "I was thinking of Brother Jephthah, who was my very first caretaker and confessor. I know he is happy now in heaven. I was thinking about him and about the many years I have labored here — boy, and now man — to be a righteous Shaker." He did not add, "and last night when I undid all those years," but it was in his thoughts.

"Fifteen, is it?" asked Sister Martha easily.

"Sixteen come Sabbath next," said Abel. He nodded at Sister Charity. "Sixteen springs. The first I witnessed from a willow basket on the Meeting House steps."

"Ah," mused Charity, smoothing her hands down over her stomach. "I have labored here near seventeen springs myself. My time in the World was much longer than that, though certainly not dearer to me."

"And I have been here over sixty years," Sister Martha said. "Faith and I came together. Our father in the World brought us as ten-year-olds when our mother died, bless him, wherever he is."

"Did you know Mother Ann then?" asked Sister Mary in a hushed voice. "Mother Ann in the flesh."

Sister Martha smiled. Her voice was low, soothing, and began to rise and fall like a chant. "Dear Sister, your numbers are amiss. We never saw Her in the flesh, Faith and I. She departed this life the year we were born. But I see Her every day. She is here with me. Always. Mother is here." She started to sing softly in her crooning voice:

> "Let names and sects and parties
> Accost my ears no more,
> My ever blessed Mother
> Forever I'll adore. . . ."

104

Abel joined in with great relief. He sang louder than all the rest. The anthem, he knew full well, had sixteen verses. They would continue singing it until Union Meeting was over. After Meeting he would have only an hour to wait before the house settled down and the Believers slept and he could go out once more and meet his Sarah.

🐚 16. Sarah

Although she had joined in the singing, mouthing words that she knew by heart, Sarah's mind was a jumble. Never had she felt this way in Union Meeting before: so far away, a distance compounded of memories and dreams. More and more, snatches of her life in the World seemed to return to her, tantalizing. She kept seeing Agatha's face, soft and loving, smiling down at her with the laughing man's hand firm on Agatha's shoulder. Were these visions sendings of the devil?

She knew she could have absented herself, pleading faintness from yesterday's beating and today's confrontation. Mother Jean was in her Union Meeting group this month. Mother Jean would surely have understood. But in the back of her mind Sarah felt she *had* to remain because of the warning in the Millennial Laws that "flesh hunters are generally willing to be absent from an orderly Union Meeting to meet their peculiar favorites in private." She was *not* a flesh hunter, nor was Abel. Her presence in Union Meeting proclaimed that. What she felt — what Abel felt — was different. It *had* to be.

Still, her thoughts were so disorderly they frightened her. She looked constantly over at Mother Jean for reassurance. But though Mother Jean had looked at her once and smiled just for her, rocking noiselessly in her chair, it had been no comfort.

Later, as the girls had prepared for sleep, Sarah had been especially quiet. The soft murmur of the others as they exchanged particulars about their Union Meetings did not intrude on Sarah's thoughts. It was only when Sister Mary touched her arm that she realized where she was.

"Sister Martha was born the year Mother Ann Lee died," Mary said. "She *almost* saw her in the flesh."

"Flesh," Sarah repeated, and the word was suddenly ugly and bitter in her mouth. She sat down on her bed abruptly and undid her bonnet strings. She took the pins from her hair and then began to brush it, remembering, as she did, Abel's hands on her head, on her arm. "Flesh!" she repeated, and she pulled the brush so fiercely through her thick hair that she brought tears to her eyes. If anyone deserved to be sent away, she thought — and not for the first time — it was she.

When the four of them were ready, lying straight in their beds, Mother Jean came in. She often came to preach them a small homily after Union Meeting.

106

Usually Sarah looked forward to it. Tonight Mother Jean looked grim.

Hands folded in front of her, she spoke quietly to them, her head nodding its own agreement. "My dear children," she said, "I am informed of a circumstance that brings me much pain."

Sarah felt cold. She was so frightened she could not move. Mother Jean knew!

"You are the youngest of the Church family and, as such, the most vulnerable of my children. Springtime sneaks up on us each year like a thief trying to steal our most precious gift, the gift of purity. I want you to consider this well."

Sarah had opened her mouth, about to confess all, when Sister Ann broke into a cry. "Oh, Mother, I did not mean it. I thought it was a gift. But I was trying to . . . she should not have told. . . ." Ann turned over on her stomach and began to sob. Every once in a while the sobbing seemed to ebb, and then a fresh burst of words would start from her again. "Such a sneak . . . I ask pardon . . . oh, oh . . ."

Mother Jean moved to her at once and sat down on the bed. She rubbed Ann's back with a slow, steady circular motion.

The other girls sat up uneasily, unable to take their eyes from the tableau.

Suddenly Sister Ann jerked around and pushed herself up on one elbow. She thrust her hand out and pointed at Sarah. *"You. You did it. You* took my dreams. You have no gift of your own and so you took mine. Took it and twisted it. *You!"* She ended on such an inarticulate note, half-word, half-sob, that she shook.

Mother Jean put her arms around Ann and

soothed. "My poor child, my poor dear child. Do not set blame. Everything will be all right. Such feelings are as common to a girl your age as the onset of the monthly flux. But we were put on this earth to overcome those feelings. To be a good Shaker is to gain control of your body and your heart. There, there. Sob it out. Cry it out. Shake it out. Then you will sleep." She held on to the weeping girl for many minutes. At last Ann fell back onto her pillow and closed her eyes, exhausted by her own emotions. Mother Jean stood up, bent over, and tucked her in. "All of you sleep. In the morning we will talk of this some more."

She blew the light out and left. As her footsteps faded down the hall, Sister Elizabeth whispered from the far wall, near the sleeping Ann. "What did she mean? What did Sister Ann mean — you stole her gift?"

Sarah whispered back, "I do not know."

Sister Mary, guessing shrewdly, said, "She probably thinks you have been reading her dream papers. Have you? And what were they about?"

Sarah said nothing.

"Oh, is that all!" said Elizabeth. There was a little laugh of dismissal in her voice. "Such a goose. She has been writing about the younger brothers. Lists and lists of their names. I have seen her scribbles as she sets them down. They are easy to read upside down. It is a silly thing to do. And then she hides them, which only makes it worse. So I told Mother this afternoon. I would not want Ann to continue the practice until she really sins."

"You? You told Mother?" Sarah smiled wryly into the dark room. *"You?"*

108

"Of course," came Elizabeth's sensible voice. "It was my duty. You would have done it, too, had you known."

"No," said Sarah with sudden understanding. "I would not have. But then, you have a gift for being open, Sister Elizabeth."

"That I do," said Elizabeth in a voice full of certainty and a total absence of guilt. "Good night."

Without meaning to, Sarah dozed, waking hours later with a start. It was still dark, but the dark had a light behind it like the dark inside the eyelids of a sleeper in a lightened room. Sarah threw her covers off and tiptoed to the window. She could see no one outside, just the black shadows of trees and the looming presence of the barn. Was Abel still waiting? Sarah hoped he would be. She *knew* he would be. If she hurried, she could explain everything to him. She would tell him all about Sister Agatha, her Worldly mother, and why she was so fierce with Sarah. And how she could never meet him, not ever again. He would understand.

"You stole my dream," came a voice from across the room.

Sarah turned. Ann was sitting up in bed.

"I stole nothing from you, Sister Ann."

"You stole my dreams and then told Mother about them," Ann whispered. "It had to be you. You were up here alone and I found one of my dreams under the bed. It was open. I know you had read it. And now I am splattered with filth."

"I told Mother nothing."

Ann's whispering continued. "I pushed you down in Meeting so that we might be even. But you told anyway."

"I know," Sarah said, realizing suddenly that she did indeed know. And understand. "I do not hate you for that." And she did not, remembering Abel's hand on her arm. "But I told Mother none of it."

"Then how did Mother know? She knew. She came in to talk to us all, but it was meant for me. And how could she know if you did not tell her?"

Sarah hesitated, thinking to name Elizabeth. But if she did, she was no better than either of them. Perhaps, in the end, her own sins were greater than theirs, but she would not add tattling to her count. "Mother knows everything," she said, and suddenly shivered. If Mother knew everything, then she *already* knew about Abel.

"She does not know everything I know," Ann said.

"What do *you* know?" Sarah was suddenly afraid. Not for herself but for Abel, waiting patiently out in the dark. She went over to Ann's bed. "What do you know?"

Ann reached up and fastened her fingers tightly around Sarah's wrist. "I know you spoke to Brother Abel. Mary told me. Spoke to a *brother*. And because I knew and had pushed you, you wanted to get even, and so you told. I will not let you go until you have confessed to me."

Sarah jerked back, but Ann's fingers had her imprisoned. She looked at Ann coldly. "I gave him a poultice for a bee sting." She was proud of not mentioning him by name. His name on her lips might betray her. "And something to ease the ache." There, she thought, only part of a lie, since he ached to talk with someone. I am getting to be very good at these half-truths. "And what would I want with one of your tatty little paper dreams, anyway?"

"They are not tatty!"

"Then why do you hide them? Why have you not shared them?" Sarah hissed, desperate to discover a way to get Ann to let go.

"I was going to. Truly I was. Only . . ."

"Only what?"

"Only I was not sure I had a gift. Not like Mary, who can speak with such ease at Meeting. Or Elizabeth, who is always so sure of herself. Or like you. I wanted to be sure of my gift first."

"Me?" Sarah was surprised. "I have no gift."

"You always say that, and it angers me so," Ann said. "You with your beautiful face. All the sisters love you. Elizabeth and Mary and Martha and Faith and especially Mother Jean. That *has* to be a gift." Ann's voice trembled. "No one even *likes* me."

Sarah, filled with sudden pity for Ann, was silent, and in the silence Ann's fingers tightened around her wrist. She pulled Sarah onto the bed next to her.

"Let me go," Sarah begged gently. "I cannot possibly *like* you if you do not let me go."

"Not unless you confess," Ann replied. "Not till then."

"I have nothing to confess." Sarah twisted her wrist.

"I think you do."

Their frenzied whispers disturbed the sleep of the other two, who began to toss and turn. Elizabeth gave a strange moaning cry. Mary curled into a tight ball.

Sarah and Ann were still for a moment, neither

111

one wanting to wake the others. But Ann's fingers never slackened their hold.

Sarah thought, She is crazed with this thing. She is consumed by some kind of invented jealousy. If I try to run off, she will certainly set up a cry. But how can I confess to something I have *not* done just to satisfy her madness? It will surely all be revealed in the morning. I must tell Abel. I must get to him and tell him that — even as friends — we must never meet again. That way he will be saved and I will be saved. And perhaps Sister Agatha will not be sent away. Sarah decided to outwait Sister Ann. When Sister Ann slept at last, Sarah would slip out of the knot of her fingers.

She tested the strength of Ann's hold once more, but she could not escape, so she tried to relax, letting herself doze and thus retain her strength. But the dark became light. Even after they had both fallen asleep, sitting upright together on the bed, Sister Ann did not let go.

☙ 17. Abel

A bel sat on the cold ground and counted the stars. There were patterns in the sky he had never seen, clusters of stars and lines, wheels of stars, and one star that moved swiftly across the sky and was gone. He had never really looked at the stars before. He wondered if the World's folks had given the stars names; he had heard they had a passion for naming useless things.

The air was crisp. There was a slight, steady breeze ruffling the trees. The sound of it through the new leaves reminded him of the sound the sisters' skirts had made, their pressed worsted rustling as they walked along the path. He rubbed his palms down the sides of his vest. They were suddenly sweaty, even though the rest of him was cold.

He breathed in deeply, and his heart seemed to echo back each breath. The smell of the air was full of the farm: cows and pigs, oven and mules, and over them all the smell of the new-turned earth.

He shivered suddenly, wondering if walking about would keep him warmer. Then, fearing to make more noise than was necessary, he huddled back into the bushes. The branches brushed against his face like busy little fingers. Soon Sarah would be there, and he would warm himself with her laugh. Just thinking about her made rivers of fire run down his legs. His stomach knotted in anticipation and there was a growing tightness in his groin. At first the physical manifestations of his feelings had frightened him. But he could no longer will them away.

He wished that he had thought to put on his coat and hat against the growing cold. He had been in too much of a hurry once the other brothers had fallen asleep. Still, Sarah would be there soon. Then they would go back to the barn. In the barn he might put his hand on hers. Friend to friend. They would share her cloak and talk till near dawn. They would not be cold.

He did not know if she could get the women's

door open. He had left the men's door slightly ajar for her. That was why he was stationed in the bushes halfway, at the midpoint between the two doors.

Putting his arms around his knees, he rehearsed how it would be. She would come out, thinking that she was walking silently along the path. But he would be up in a moment and surprise her. Then she would move toward him as swiftly as the star had moved across the sky. He would touch her hair again. "My only friend," he would say. "My wife." And then she would understand. She would look up at him with the perfect heart-shaped face. She would answer, "My friend. My husband, Abel." That was how they would be married at first — in God's sight. They would have to leave New Vale, of course. But that would be all right. They could get a farm down in the valley. Brother Joshua would know what to do. He could even move in with them, to help with the farming. They would have children whom they would love and cherish and keep. It would be a good, good life. He could not wait to tell her.

The owl, calling from a maple tree, woke him the first time. He had no idea how long he had slept. Along the horizon he could see the gray line of the false dawn. He stood up, stiff and cold, and tried to get his body to move properly. His stomach felt tight, as if he had eaten something bitter.

He wondered why Sarah was not there yet, but he was not overly concerned. She might have had to wait longer for the sisters in her room to fall asleep. Unless she had decided not to come because he was such a fool. The scene in the dining hall came back to him again, and his face flushed with the memory.

114

He tiptoed down the path to the men's door. It was as he had left it. Turning around, he went back to his lookout. After a few minutes of standing, he sat back under the bushes again. The branches enfolded him like an old friend.

The second time he awoke, it was dawn. Gray and lonely and cold. He thought about the days that now seemed to stretch endlessly ahead of him. If he wanted to, he could think of any number of explanations for Sarah's absence. *Any* number. Only why should he try? The only one who was important to him now was himself. He knew what he had to do. He would work hard. Harder than he had ever worked before. He would not let himself be filled with anger. He would not let himself be filled with hate. He would keep an empty place inside and let nothing come into it. He would especially not let himself cry.

But his tongue found an escaped tear at the corner of his mouth as he glanced back toward the women's door. He walked down the path. Heedless now of any noise he might be making, he went through the men's door and let it slam. He took the stairs slowly, savoring every creak. But no one noticed. No one was listening. No one heard. In his room the others greeted his return with snores. He undressed and crawled under the covers, forcing himself to lie very straight. He would not think about her. He would never again say her name. But it came to him, moments later, in a dream: Sarah.

115

May 1, 1854

❧ 18. Sarah

The first day of May was full and fair. Onions had long since sent their green messages up through the soil of the vegetable gardens. Soon spinach and peas, radishes and carrots, pumpkins and squash and summer sarse would go in.

From the herb gardens where she was helping transplant hyssop and feverfew, Sarah watched Father James move up and down the straight rows of vegetables, nodding contentedly at the order around his feet. Sarah covered a yawn with a hand that smelled of herbs. It was such a fresh, pure scent she wanted to cry.

When she had awakened at dawn, still pinioned by Sister Ann's fingers, Sarah *had* wept. Then she had pried loose Ann's grip with ease, but she knew it was much too late. Looking out of the window, with every tree and bush outlined by the golden dawn, she was not surprised that Abel could not be seen. He had probably left hours earlier, when it had become clear that she was not going to come.

She wondered how she might explain it to him, excuse it to him, make up to him his long, cold vigil. If only they might meet alone by chance along the garden paths. But she knew sisters had to go everywhere by twos. Brothers as well. Perhaps they could whisper undetected across the dining hall. But it might as well be miles between them there. Perhaps she could spin close enough to him at Meeting, crying out some phrase as if in a trance, a phrase that he would understand one way but any listener could not uncode. She tried out several sentences in her mind: "I could not come to Meeting, yet I want to go to Meeting." Was it too obvious? "This is a Meeting of the Light — when is a Meeting in the dark?" But that suggested they were aligned with the powers of darkness. And she did not mean such a thing. All the sentences she could think of were too long and cumbersome, either too clear or not clear enough. She discarded the idea.

When she had finished a row, Sarah stood up and went over to Sister Tabit to get more plants. As she prized apart the roots, Sister Tabit remarked, "You seem to have a gift for gardening, child. In the next few days Mother and I will be moving the horehound and sage. We will want your help then as well."

"Yes, Sister," Sarah answered distractedly. She had just caught sight of several brothers working across the road in the west orchards, the newly cleared land behind the white clapboard Meeting House. As one brother in particular stood up, stretched, and then bent over again to set in another of the hundreds of

117

small apple and pear trees that were being planted, Sarah thought she recognized Abel. But it was too far away to tell for sure. He might not be in the orchard at all. Perhaps he was with the party of brethren checking out the wild sarsaparilla root. Or in the barn where, according to Sister Phoebe, who did spring milking, Apostle was close to her time. It was hopeless to believe she could speak to Brother Abel alone outside. She did not even know where he was. She sighed.

"Are you doing too much bending today, Sister?" said Mother Jean, walking over to them. She threaded her way along the garden with ease. After so many years she knew where each herb was planted. "Does your back still ache?"

"Yes, Mother. No, Mother." Sarah was not sure which answer was correct. Her back ached slightly, but something inside her ached even more.

"They say work heals all ills," said Mother Jean.

"I thought that was time," Sister Tabit added with a laugh.

"Yes, that, too," Mother Jean said. "Time *and* work heal all ills. Well I know it."

"All ills," Sarah repeated.

"I think that you should work indoors this afternoon," Mother Jean said, musing. "No more bending or stretching. Help the sisters in the kitchen."

"The kitchen sisters?" Sarah's voice sounded weak, thin.

"Mother, forgive me questioning your decision," Sister Tabit interrupted. Her long association with Mother Jean and her position as eldress allowed her such privileges, which she always softened with an excuse. "I know you are prompted by concern. But

118

do you think, in this instance, that the *kitchen* is quite the place for her?"

"I would have you bear in mind a caution as you work, my child," Mother Jean said to Sarah, though it was clear from what followed that she was answering Sister Tabit as well. "In the World we were fond of saying that you can catch flies with honey sooner than vinegar. But I would say rather that, when you are on a straight path, it is best not to look too far behind or too far ahead. Concentrate your mind on the place where your feet are stepping. And trust that Mother will lead you in safety." She touched Sarah's cheek briefly with her cool hand. "Do you think you can do that?"

Sarah nodded, and at that moment the dinner bell rang.

She did not know why she was not hungry. Usually she had a hearty appetite, and today's meal — fish and dandelion greens, with dried apple pie for dessert — was a favorite of hers. She took tiny portions and could scarcely get them down. It was if spring, instead of quickening her, had turned her stomach sour and her appetite small. Perhaps it was the sight of Abel's back, his head held high, his shoulders squared, sitting at the table across from hers. Each time she looked up, she could feel a pain in her stomach. She had not been able to speak to him in line or even acknowledge him with a look. But sometime, soon, she promised herself, she would surely find a way.

What was more immediate were the first words she would speak to Sister Agatha in the kitchen. Though she minded Mother Jean's words about the honey and vinegar, about recalling the past or summoning the future, she knew that if she could choose just the right words, then she and Sister Agatha might find some measure of peace with one another. She remembered again the gentler dream face and the gentler tone of her mother's singing with great longing. Not that they ever could be *that* way again, mother and daughter. After all, *that* was in the World and therefore sinful, and besides, it was far in the past. But surely they might recapture the feelings that had occasionally sprung up between them when they had clung to one another in Meeting.

Sarah rose with the others at the meal's end, leaving the solemn line only when they passed the kitchen door.

"I am here at Mother's prompting to do your bidding, Sisters," she announced quietly.

The seven sisters looked up from their tasks, and Sister Charity, who ran the kitchen, nodded. She was a large, homely woman with one bad eye that wandered. She also had a gift for pastry. She was, it was said by visiting Believers, the best baker in all the Shaker kitchens.

"Help Margaret and Rachel set the tables aright," said Sister Charity. "And bring in all the serving dishes. After that, Agatha will need your help with the pans. Fifteen apple pies and that blamed fish make for a great deal of extra work, much as we all enjoy them, praise the Lord's bounty. You can scrape and Agatha can wash. Then you can dry. Bless Mother for sending you."

Sarah smiled at Sister Charity's words. The kitchen sister was known for her colorful blending of blessings and curses, and all the years she had lived as a Shaker had not curbed her tongue.

"I will help gladly," Sarah answered, keeping her eyes down on her own hands, folded properly before her.

"Then hop to," said Sister Charity. "And praise be for you."

Agatha grunted a grudging acceptance of the arrangements, but said nothing more.

When the tables and benches were straightened and Margaret and Rachel at work with their brooms, Sarah came back into the kitchen. It was moist with the steam rising from the soapy water in the sinks. Three sisters worked around one double sink, washing and drying the dishes and mugs and putting them away carefully on the well-constructed shelving. Sister Charity bustled about the chopping table, clearing away the remains of food and storing things in clearly marked crocks. Her thoughts were already quite obviously on the preparation for the next meal. Agatha, her sleeves rolled up past her elbows, stood over the largest sink. A single strand of escaping hair crossed her forehead like a moving scar. Sarah longed to tuck that hair gently under Agatha's white cap, but she did not. Instead, without a word, she walked to the sink and began to scrape the pie plates into the slop bucket.

"Here, do it this way," said Agatha, taking a plate from Sarah's hand. She showed her how to loosen the stubborn crusts without damaging the surface of the plate, then thrust the half-scraped tin back at Sarah.

121

They worked side by side in silence for a long while before Sarah finally decided on the proper words. "Your way is easier," she said at last.

"Perhaps not easier, but better," Agatha answered.

Sarah was suddenly aware that they were not talking about pots and pans, but about something else. "Can't they . . . sometimes be the same?" she asked.

"The easy road is the devil's own," said Agatha shortly. Then she added with a strange look on her face, "Though sometimes it seems the more loving."

Sarah jumped on the word. "Loving. But that is what we Shakers talk about. Loving. How can that be wrong? Can the devil love?"

"The devil is a *man!*" Agatha fairly shouted the word.

Sarah scrubbed at the pie plate without looking up, her cheeks flushed with the effort not to retort, to say that Father James was a man, and Brother Eben, and all the brothers at New Vale. At last she said, as quietly as she could, "Sister, I do not want to quarrel with you. Not ever. I just want to ask . . ."

"Go to your *Mother,*" said Sister Agatha angrily. "That is what Mother is for." She hesitated and then added, "It is not for men to decide who is to be a mother. That is for God to decide. Mother Jean is God's chosen Mother here. Go to Mother Jean with your questions. *She* is your Mother just as she is mine."

Sarah felt tears starting. "I just wanted you to guide me. As in the song. Remember?" And she began to hum the cradle song, inserting the two lines she could remember.

> *"I will guard thee,*
> *I will guide thee . . ."*

Agatha responded to the line in a crooning voice that Sarah only vaguely recognized as the one from her dream, for Agatha's voice was harsher than the dream voice.

> *"When the nighttime*
> *Comes to hide thee.*
>
> *I will rock thee,*
> *I will shield thee,*
> *Till the daylight*
> *Comes to heal . . .*

I will sing that no more." Agatha broke off sharply. "It is not a Shaker hymn, and it is better not to recall what is past. There is evil in the past. Great evil. Only here, in the present, in New Vale, is there good. And safety." She set her lips together in that thin grimace that Sarah had come to recognize and fear.

Sarah took up another pan, scraping it furiously, and said nothing more until broad grace set her free. Then she slipped gratefully into her place on the bench and schooled her thoughts along Shaker lines, wondering only briefly what *great evil* was in the past that kept Agatha prisoned here.

May 7, 1854

❧ 19. Abel

Abel tried to squeeze a month's worth of work into a week. He refused the easier chores given to those who had finished the heaviest labors, and volunteered for even more arduous tasks. He worked mornings in the orchard, setting out the hundreds of small apple and pear trees, never complaining about a stiff back, even reveling in it. He went a second time onto Holy Hill to help hand-trim the grass. With a hand scythe he mowed down nearly six acres of meadow land. Then he plowed it in winter wheat, wrestling with the pair of lethargic oxen who were less interested in pulling the plow than in the grass on either side of them.

At Meetings he sang louder than his neighbors. He boomed out the words of hymns as if strength of voice equaled strength of purpose. He simply worked himself and prayed himself into a stupor so that late at night, when he lay straight-limbed in his bed, he thought only of sleep and nothing more.

Father James even commented to him in the hallway one morning, "You see, I was right. The footsteps in the hallway have ceased. A father can *always* tell when one of his children is troubled. But work cures all. Work and the will to follow your father's way. Bend with me, boy, or you will be broken. But I was right, was I not?"

Abel bowed his head and walked out to the barn. There he threw himself into his next labor. He did not think of himself as following Father James's advice but Mother Ann Lee's dictum. His hands were surely given over to work. But his heart felt almost dead inside his chest. True, he had seen Sister Sarah a few times — in the dining hall, across the room at Meeting, once on the walkway ahead of him. And each time, his heart had seemed to stutter. So he took to looking down at his feet whenever he walked where a woman might pass. In that way he would not even *see* her if she went by.

At the end of the week Brother Joshua and Brother Jackson returned. Abel was sent to help them unload. It was the first of the "lesser" tasks he had accepted with any degree of enthusiasm. He closed the gate after the wagon, then trotted to catch up with it.

"I am to help," he called up to the two. They looked tired. Joshua took off his broad-brimmed hat, swatting at it with his fingers. Little clouds of road dust ballooned into the air. Brother Jackson coughed, then jumped down.

"It is good to be home again," he said. "I even prefer New Vale dust to the roads of the big towns." He coughed and smiled, as if to emphasize his point. Then he went around to the back of the wagon.

Abel held a hand up to Brother Joshua. The older man took it gratefully. "Sitting such a long time aggravates this leg of mine," he said. "And you, boy, how did you fare while I was gone?" He asked it quietly, staring into Abel's face. "You looked peaked. The spring jimjams?"

"That is over," Abel said. "Done with. Finished."

"Said once, with a smile, and I would believe you. Said three times, with a face like sour apples, and it makes a man wonder." Joshua pursed his lips. Then he clapped his hand on Abel's shoulder. "But we will talk later. Right now we need to get the wagon unloaded and the horse into the barn and fed."

They worked swiftly, bringing the heavy bags of sugar and salt and other goods that could not be made or grown at New Vale into the kitchen for the sisters to sort. Then Brother Jackson sought out Elder Eben and Father James to give them the money and letters from the trip. Joshua and Abel walked the horse and wagon into the barn.

For the first time in a week the barn seemed like an old friend to Abel. It was cool and inviting again, not simply a place to labor in. He drew in a deep breath.

They unhitched the horse. Abel led her back down the driveway to the lower barn while Joshua checked over the wagon wheels. He had suspected one needed mending.

Abel fed the horse and settled her in the barn. He

promised her a chance to kick up her heels the next day in the pasture.

"And you, too, by the look of it, could do with some heel-kicking, boy. What ails you?" Joshua was suddenly at his side.

"I *was* sick," said Abel slowly, "but now I am healed."

"Scarred, more likely," said Joshua with a small smile.

"Please, Joshua, do not laugh at me. I could not stand it."

Joshua put his head on the horse's flank. "Laugh, boy? I have never laughed *at* you. Have you never here the saying, 'He jests at scars that never felt a wound'? My mother said it often."

"No, I never heard it."

"Well, it is true, boy. I would not laugh at you. No more than you would laugh at me. But we can both laugh at ourselves. *That* is something Father James could never do." He gave the horse a few soft pats and signaled Abel out of the stall. "I have to go and wash up from the trip. Besides, I think that must be the supper bell. And I am hungry as a bear. Except for a good Shaker meal at Harvard — where they serve a mighty fine tomato soup — we ate scanty most days. I sure do miss Sister Charity's pies."

They washed together and went in. Broad grace time gave Abel a chance to think about Joshua's homecoming. With the old man's return, Abel could feel the hardness around his heart softening. He could breathe easier. And taking several experimental deep breaths, Abel smiled. For the first time in a week he closed his eyes and really prayed.

❧ 20. Sarah

I t was the eve of the Mountain Feast. Even Sarah was excited. In the retiring room none of the girls had spoken as they dressed in their Sabbath clothes, though Ann, who had not said a word to Sarah for a week, managed a faint nod in her direction. Mary had been wreathed in smiles all day, and Elizabeth hummed as she tied her cap strings. It was a happy, tuneless hum. Walking out of the room next to Elizabeth, Sarah felt a kind of magic in the air. She crossed and recrossed her thumbs until she noticed what she was doing, then willed herself to be calm.

The line of women threaded its way down the stairs, through the hall, and into the dining room. As she entered the room, which was stripped as usual for Meeting, Sarah felt the difference in spirit at once. Shadows danced nimbly along the walls, bowing and bending to the tune of the many flickering candles. She waited patiently in the line, Elizabeth next to her calm and unmoving, and she tried not to think about anything. She especially tried not to think about Abel. Yet she knew he was near, across the room, waiting as she waited for the ceremony to begin.

128

Slowly the line moved forward, one step, two steps, then a halt. Hands folded against her stomach, Sarah concentrated on counting her breaths. Fifty-nine, sixty, then another step. Sixty-seven, sixty-eight, then another step. At last, though, it was her turn. And Elizabeth's.

They took two steps forward and knelt. In front of them, half in shadow, half in light, stood Mother Jean and Father James. Eldress Tabit and Elder Eben flanked them. Between the standing men and women was a space — and yet not a space. It was a spiritual chest of drawers. Sarah knew it was there because she had been told it was there. Her first Mountain Eve at New Vale she had said, in her high child's voice that had carried across the room, "But there is *nothing* there." The next time, in September, she had thrown herself into the imaginary game with great enthusiasm, swearing to the other children in the Gathering Order that not only had she seen the chest, but it had golden handles and silver keyholes and a special drawer that had gems spelling out "Only for Sarah Barker" on its side. Sister Agatha's switch had soon cured her of that. "Take care you do not develop a gift for lying," Sister Agatha had warned. "Lies sit heavy in the heart." And, oh, how right she was.

The following feast days Sarah had stood in line and had seen nothing. And had said nothing. But she had finally come to understand that it was neither a game nor a reality but something in between.

As Sarah knelt, she looked up at Mother Jean, who was bending over the shadow chest and moving her hands as if pulling out rolls of fabric. Mother

Jean straightened up and handed an invisible garment, one to Elizabeth and then one to Sarah.

Sarah held out her hands to receive the dress. Then she put on the unseen garment with the help of an equally invisible angel. She found herself smiling indulgently at the dumb show and wondering how it all would look to an outsider. Then, bowing the requisite four low bows, she turned.

In turning, she found herself face to face with Abel, who stood looking back at her across the shadow-filled room. Startled, she did not look down but instead held out her hand in a slight, involuntary gesture. Her eyes felt hot and prickly, as if she were going to cry. She could not read his expression in the flickering light, but he looked away quickly and walked out the men's door. Without stopping, Sarah continued her turn and marched out the women's door.

"Did you feel Mother Ann there? I know she was one of the angels. I *know* it." It was Mary, right behind her, in a soft whisper.

"I felt nothing," Sarah said. *"Nothing."*

Stunned by the force of Sarah's denial, Mary turned for comfort to Ann, who stood by her side, but Mary was even more appalled by the look of triumph on Ann's face.

"If you would confess," Ann whispered, *"'then* you could feel again."

"I have nothing to confess to *you*," said Sarah angrily. Pushing her chin out and holding her head high, she marched past the others and up the stairs.

The other girls trailed behind her in silence all the way back to the room.

* * *

In the morning Sarah steadfastly refused to talk to any of the others, dressing silently in both her real and her spiritual garments. She ate her breakfast mechanically and helped sweep the hall in the same mechanical way. When she took her place in the women's line, part of what Mary kept calling their "shining company," Sarah did not smile or nod at the others. Her face stern, as if she were walking on the edge of a precipice, she trudged after the others outside and up Holy Hill. In her pocket was a note of fevered explanation to Brother Abel, telling him about Sister Agatha and about Sarah's decision never to meet him again, though, as the note said, "In my heart I will remain your sister and your friend." She had written it guided only by a sliver of moonlight after the others had slept. She knew she had to find a moment during the Mountain Feast, when the brothers and sisters would all be together and it would be natural to slip the note into Abel's hand. She owed him that. And she owed it to her own peace.

Her mood did not communicate to the others. They remained afire with the joy of the coming celebration. Their steps were jaunty, their faces eager.

Halfway up Holy Hill, near the place where Sarah had hidden, crouched in the bushes like a frightened hare, the marchers gathered into one large circle to hear whatever spirits chose to speak to them.

Sarah reached into her pocket and drew out the paper. If she could, she would speak out and move close enough to Abel to pass it on. Next to her, on her left, Elizabeth trembled with anticipation.

131

On her right, Sister Ann moved restlessly from one foot to the other.

The silence in the circle stretched on.

Suddenly Sister Charity began speaking in a strange voice, much deeper and more cultured than her usual tones. She had a foreign-sounding accent and spoke rapidly. "I am General Lafayette," she said. "I have come to tell *mes amis* that in the spirit world the war between good and evil is still being waged. But with the help of the angels who live in the world and call themselves the United Society of Believers in the First and Second Appearing of Christ, the good *shall* prevail. I urge you, *mes amis,* to fight. Fight the serpent in you. Fight." She finished by raising her arm and lowering her head.

Around the circle others followed her gesture. And then the praises and blessings began. Many spoke just a sentence or a phrase, as if impelled to call out their testimony by the beauty of the spring day. Brother Frank, tickled by a laughing spirit, giggled his way through an old prayer, and the words of the prayer seemed to take on a new and even more blessed meaning. Sister Faith gave them a message from Pocahontas. Two older brothers spoke antiphonally, one asking questions, the other giving answers, as if they were a father and child.

Suddenly a soft, melodious voice overrode them all. "Mother's dove is flying over our circle now." It was Sister Mary, her dark face shiny with sweat, though the day was on the cool side. Her eyes were wide open, darting around the circle as if following the erratic flight of a bird.

132

The others watched with her.

"There, there it flies. And there. And there," she continued, pointing. Then, holding out her hand, she said, "See how it settles in my hand. So pure. So white. And it tells me. "What?" She brought her hand to her ear and stood a moment, listening. Then she smiled broadly. "It says it has brought me something for one of the Believers to wear up to the Fountain. See?" She picked something from her hand and shook it out. Then slowly she walked around the inside of the circle, passing quickly by the brothers. At last she stopped in front of Sarah and swung the invisible garment over Sarah's shoulders. "It is Mother's cloak," she said. "It will keep you safe."

Sarah tried not to feel anything, but a sudden warmth enveloped her. Surprised, she unclenched her fists and then slowly brought her hands up to her shoulders. She could almost feel the scratchy surface of a wool cloak there. Standing still, she closed her eyes and whispered. "Thank you, dear Sister Mary. I *do* feel safe now."

Mary's answer stayed with her the rest of the way up the hill. "Do not thank me. Thank Mother Ann. She wants your happiness. That is all."

133

❧ 21. Abel

The circle broke apart. The two separate lines reformed easily. Then the marchers began to climb Holy Hill once again.

Abel could not shake the vision of Sarah's face, first in the candle shadow of the evening when he had turned from her, and now in the morning light with Mother's invisible cloak on her shoulders. As she had taken the cloak, she had dropped something to the ground. Something small and white. Like a piece of crumpled paper. A small sin dropping from her as easily as that. In the mood of the day Abel suddenly realized that if he gave her only sorrow and Mother only joy, he should not take Sarah away. She had been right to fear him. She had been right to stay away from him. And he had been wrong to be hurt by her decision. Love, he thought, should be manifest in joy. He would do only what was best for Sarah.

And then the marchers rounded the last turn of the Hill. Abel felt the warring passions of the last week drop away from him as easily as that little white paper sin had dropped from Sarah's hand.

He reveled once again in the felling of *rightness* here on the mountainside. The well-tended grounds welcomed them all with green praises. Seven of the finest singers — who had been practicing for days — gathered at the head of the marchers. They turned and sang beautifully:

> *"To the Fountain Stone we are going*
> *With our voices sounding shrill,*
> *And our hearts unite in praises*
> *While we mount this holy hill."*

Then Sister Tabit, as the Eldress, walked around the entire company, swinging an invisible censer. Abel did not know where the scent of spring on Holy Hill ended and the spirit incense began. He only knew that everything smelled sweet and fresh and new. He threw his hands into the air and gave a great happy shout and was answered back by the entire company. The dance had begun.

No two brothers or sisters acted together. Each one danced independently. Brother Andrew marched up and down, clapping his hands and singing. Jonas jogged a few tentative steps, then hopped up and down. Jacob contented himself with a kind of twisting, swaying, wavering. Brother John turned cartwheel after cartwheel until he was dizzy and had to sit. He continued to roll around on the grass afterward. The older brethren danced as well. Brother Eben waltzed slowly with his stick as a partner, in a kind of half-memory of his youth in the World. Even Joshua rocked back and forth, one leg to another, though he did not stay long on the lame leg. He looked, Abel thought fondly, a bit like a self-conscious old bear just up from its wintering. Abel went over and put his arms around Joshua. For a moment they rocked together.

The opening dance lasted only a short time. Abel was glad of it, for he knew they had a long day ahead. First would come the spirit bathing in the great white tubs filled with spiritual water from the Fountain Stone. The invisible water was supposed to wash them clean. But, Abel wondered, how could he feel any cleaner, any fresher, any purer than he felt already?

Next they would each drink a deep draught of spiritual wine and throw fool at one another. He smiled, remembering the last feast, a warm September day. He and Andrew had gotten so drunk on the invisible wine that they had crawled on their hands and knees, mooing and lowing like cows. Foolish as they had been, they had not been half as merry as Brother Jackson. He had wandered all around the Fountain Stone, crowing like a sunstruck rooster. Only Father James contained himself, never throwing fool, only standing apart and smiling indulgently at them all, a father enjoying his foolish children.

The sun passed its zenith and was beginning its descent when Abel's stomach growled dangerously. After all the singing and dancing and throwing fool, he was getting hungry. He knew that he should not let the real world intrude on the Mountain Feast, but he could not seem to control his own insides. And he also knew the only food he would be getting for the next several hours would be heavenly fare. Apples and pears, pineapples and plums, cherries and sweet cakes, and flagons of wine. Invisible and filling to the soul. But surely not enough to make a stomach stop its noise. The brothers and sisters would spend an hour gathering the spirit food from the trees that bordered the Fountain Stone plot.

As he helped with the harvest, Abel felt himself slip in and out of the scene. A part and yet apart. One minute he could almost feel the fruit, soft, plump, inviting. The next his fingers closed on air. One minute he joined the gatherers, singing mightily. The next he watched strangers in an elaborate farce. He had never felt this way before. He wondered if this was to be his *real* punishment. Surely a good Shaker should not feel this way. Angry with his lack of concentration, ashamed of his past sins — much larger and darker than Sarah's — and fearful of a future without promise, Abel shouted out louder than the rest. When they sat at the invisible tables, passing invisible danties first to the elders and the ministry and then to the common members, he murmured again and again at the beauty of the fruit. He remarked on its juiciness. Its tastiness. The gift each bite contained.

He tried to recall his earlier mood, when he had seen the little sin dropping away from Sarah's hand. It had looked so real — why did the fruit not look that way? That little paper sin drifting out of her hand. Crumpled. Discarded. In an agony he suddenly smote his hand to his thigh. It was an overdramatic gesture that no one noticed. The paper had looked real because it *was* real. Paper sin, in-

137

deed. It had been a *real piece of paper*. Tangible evidence. She had dropped a note. For him. He was sure of it. And if the note was real, its existence proved she cared for him. Proved she dared for him. He would find the note — and find a way to respond.

Sister Tabit and Brother Eben were speaking in the voices of angels, passing up and down the tables. They chanted, "More zeal, more zeal, more life, more fervency, more energy, more love, more thankfulness, more obedience, more strength, more power."

I will give them more, Abel thought. And out loud he sang, *"Amen!"* with such vigor that he even startled himself. "Amen," he repeated. His voice seemed so filled with new joy that some of the others answered him, "Amen."

He looked at the faces around the men's table as he said each amen. They were open and trusting and believing. It was his chance to let Sarah know that he knew. He stood up.

"Amen," he sang out, walking over to Jacob and Jonas. To Andrew and John.

They nodded, singing back, "Amen."

"Amen," he sang to brother after brother, and even Brother Joshua, who usually eschewed showy responses, nodded at him. "Amen."

He dared to look at the sisters openly. "Amen," he said, walking to within five feet of them. At the Mountain Feast, spurred on by a gift of thanksgiving, such boldness would be allowed. He smiled at Mother Jean and Sister Tabit. They sang back to him, harmoniously, "Amen."

"Amen," sang Sister Faith and Martha together.

138

One by one they answered. Black Mary ecstatically. Elizabeth with solemnity. "Amen."

Then he came to Sarah.

"Amen." His voice was expectant.

She stared at him. There was a moment of silence as she missed the beat. Her mouth went all awry.

She knows, he thought at first. She understands. But when she did not answer, his certainty bled away from him. He continued to smile, but there was little hope left in it. He moved on to the last of the sisters and sang a careful "Amen."

Tremulously, Sister Ann smiled. She put her hand out as if to touch him, then drew it back. "Amen," she answered. Then she sang it a second time, stealing Sarah's lost answer. "Amen." Somehow there was a sound of triumph in it.

Then the feast was over. Abel stood with the rest. He marched with them once around the Fountain Stone. Then, four abreast, two brothers and two sisters, they went back down the hillside, singing:

> *"I will march, I will go*
> *In this pretty shining way*
> *In freedom's lovely valley*
> *On my organ I will play."*

He never heard the words. His eyes were busy scanning the hillside in a last forlorn desire to find the paper. But by the time they reached the bottom of the mountain, he had come to the conclusion that the paper, like his hopes, had either been blown away by an invisible wind or had never existed except in his mind.

☙ 22. Meeting

The remainder of the afternoon and early evening the Dwelling House hummed with the sisters' work. Every one of them had been summoned to finish the labor of cleaning that had been begun in the invisible white tubs on Holy Hill. Windows were removed and scrubbed till the glass panes shimmered. The plain woven carpets were beaten thoroughly. The floors were lovingly polished. And all the while, Mother Ann Lee's words, spoken so long ago, were passed along in greeting: "There is no dirt in heaven. Good spirits will not dwell where there is dust."

As Sarah scrubbed and polished, her hands were busy but her mind had too much time to think. She dwelt on images of Abel: when he had lifted her up at Meeting, the chance encounter in the Nurse Shop, his moonlit face on the garden path at midnight, his voice telling secrets in the barn, and that very afternoon on Holy Hill when his eyes on her had put the lie to his amens. She had seen it from the shelter of Mother Ann's cloak. But now she wondered if she really wanted to be sheltered. One part of her did, wanted to be kept warm until the end of her life, safe in the love of the community. But another part of her wanted to dare to shake off the cloak and walk again in the moonlight with Brother Abel by her side.

In the barn, where the brethren were cleaning the stalls and wagons and animals as carefully as they had cleansed their souls, Abel labored. Where there is work, he mused, there is not thought. When the body is tired, it will sleep without dreams. If he feared anything now, it was the thought of dreaming. He worked at a feverish pitch.

In the kitchen Sister Agatha scrubbed until her knuckles were sore, cleaning every single pot from the pantry shelves two and three times over. As she worked, she tried to scrub her mind free of the scene on the mountaintop where that brother, that *boy,* had stepped in front of Sister Sara. Oh, he had sung a simple amen that may have fooled the others. But he had not fooled her. His mouth had cried the innocent, but his eyes had been burning. Burning. She knew that look. Had seen it often enough in the World. It was the mark of desire. How could Sara have not recognized it? She was Satan's daughter, born of carnality. Her father communicated his lust to everything he touched. But God had punished her with dead babies. Until she acknowledged His revelation and ran away from the devil. Put him far, far behind her. If she scrubbed and scrubbed, some of the remaining stain might rub away. Some of her own stain. And her daughter Sara's.

The bell summoned the Believers to the Sabbath Eve Meeting, cutting across retiring time with its loud authority. Those who were gossipy stilled their tongues. Those who were sleepy shook themselves awake.

In two careful lines they paraded down the stairs and, with the precision of dancers, came into the dining hall.

Forming opposing ranks, sisters on the left, breathren on the right, they were still for just a moment. Shoulders were squared. Hands were carefully folded, right thumb over left. The silence deepened as they waited for the cue to begin.

Then Mother Jean began, singing the first line of the hymn "All That." Her voice was accompanied by the metronomic nodding of her head. Her face was clear, untroubled.

"Though many foes beset me round," she began.

The rest entered on the second line. There were, of course, no stragglers.

> *"My self and pride and all that*
> *Yet since the way of life I've found*
> *I'll bear my cross for all that*
> *For all that and all that*
> *My hatred strife and all that*
> *The noble soul that's truly wise*
> *Will trample soon on all that."*

It was Mother Jean's favorite hymn, as Robert Burns, the World's poet, who had written the original song, had been her favorite poet years before. She had long ago forgotten the other words.

When the three verses were done, the Believers continued standing. The building was still ringing with their sound when Father James began to speak.

"And I say to you that if you be a doubting Thomas, like Thomas Brown of old, you will come, as he did, to nothing. Turn your back on the way of God, and God will turn his back on you. Yet you will have a residue of that true faith, and it will be an eternal torment to you. Better to have never entered Eden than to leave it. Better to be always of the World than return to it. Better never to see the face of God than to see it only in your memory." Instead of flushing with the effort of speaking, Father James grew pale. His face seemed bleached of all human color, leeched of everything but the Word.

"Oh, God," whispered Sarah, beginning to tremble.

The women on either side of her, not realizing why she had spoken, used her words as a chorus. "Oh, God, Good, God," they sang, expecting her to sing it back.

Sarah was silent.

Abel closed his eyes. He knew that Father James was speaking directly to him. He tried to make his thoughts clear, but they seemed to swim around in his head as muddy as a river in spring flood. When he opened his eyes he was staring straight at Sarah. He looked away reluctantly.

Someone began singing a mortification song. The singer had a tuneless voice, but others took up the song and carried it to a sweeter note. Abel sang along with them.

"I hate my pride, deceit, and lust.
I'll war with them forever,
I know of God they are accurst
And every good Believer."

Abel turned back and looked again at Sarah. He could not read her expression, but as he watched, she held up her hands as if pleading with him. Pointedly, he looked down at his own hands, held rigidly before him, and continued to sing, louder than before, but it did not make him feel any better.

"No peace with them I'll ever make,
They doomed to desolation,
Against them now I want to shake,
Shake with indignation."

At the last lines several women began to follow the words, shaking their hands and then their arms in an exaggeration of palsy. They shook their entire bodies, singing again as they did so, "Against them now I want to shake, shake with indignation."

"Shake, shake, shake," Brother Frank boomed out, stepping forward a pace and following his words with action.

Soon the entire family was crying out, "Shake, shake, shake." Without further instruction, they moved into another short hymn, "Shake, shake, Shaker life," marching in two concentric circles around the room. Everyone moved except Sarah and — behind her and to the right, like a shadow self — Sister Ann. They stood still, a calm eye in the center of the whirling storm. Sarah held her hands by her side, staring at the place where Abel

144

had been, as if coming to a decision. Ann's hands were in her pockets, but her body was as tense as a cat on the prowl.

As the hymn began to wind down, quieting, subsiding into a hum, Ann moved forward. "There is something I must say," she cried loudly. Then, when the whirling sisters had stopped, many breathing heavily, and the brethren slowed as well, Ann said more softly, "There is something I know."

The room was silent, as if even the benches were listening.

"This something was to have been a secret. But secrets are not the Shaker way." Her right hand came out of her pocket, clutched in a fist. She shook it at Sarah.

"I have told nothing," Sarah said.

"But I shall," Ann replied. She opened her hand slowly, and in the palm was a crumpled piece of paper. With the fingers of her left hand, she slowly smoothed it open. "This is not *my* 'tatty little paper dream,'" said Ann. "It is yours. Shall I read it aloud?"

"Read it," came a man's voice from the rear.

"Yes, read it," several voices urged.

"No!" Sarah cried and simultaneously made a swipe at Ann's hand. The paper dropped to the floor, and before Ann could recover it, Mother Jean's foot was over it.

"It is about a man," said Ann viciously.

"It is about me," said Sarah, and turned her back on Ann as if dismissing her. Slowly she started around the room, looking. Abel raised his head, ready to meet her eyes, but she passed him. Sister Agatha stood slightly apart, her cheeks burning with two red spots. Sarah moved up to her and spoke directly. "I wrote what I wrote for you."

"No," whispered Agatha. "No. Never."

"Because all I ever wanted to know was *why*. Why must the past be forgotten? Why must past love be forgotten?"

Agatha whispered. "The man must be forgotten. He was evil."

Sarah shook her head. "But what *I* remember is not evil. He was a laughing man. A gentle man. A hardworking, loving man. What is the evil in that? What had to be forgotten? What has to be forgiven?" She spoke of her father, but she was speaking of Abel as well.

Agatha twisted her head away and spat on the floor. "Thus and thus I refute you. Thus and thus."

"But I do not, I cannot refute you, my own true blood mother," said Sarah. "And the note was about that as well."

There was a muttering from the Believers around her, but Sarah plunged ahead, her heart pounding.

"I claim kinship. I *am* yours. I know the father of my blood is dead. But you and I are bone of the same bone, too. Blood of the same blood. Say it. Please, Mother, please say it."

Agatha drew herself up. "You are no child of mine. I never wanted you. Only *he* did," she said hoarsely. "I was Agatha Lanyard. Do you see? Do you not all see it? *Agatha Lanyard*. But my father gave me away to him, to Satan, to Abraham Barker. And so I was Agatha Lanyard no more. It did not matter to them that I wanted to remain pure in my father's home. They forced me. They said it was my duty. But how can *that* be duty that horses and cows and pigs do, but angels do not?" She turned and held her hands up, pleading, looking into the faces of the sisters one at a time, as if seeking understanding. Then her voice dropped. "And I liked it. Dear Mother, I *enjoyed* it. I waited for him to come to our marriage bed each night. I became more insatiable than Satan. And he laughed when I conceived a child. Said it would give him some rest.

"And then there were the babies. One and two and three dead before her —" She pointed to Sarah with a shaking finger. "And after her, one more dead. I wanted none of them. Just him. And when they died, I was glad of it. *Glad.* But you lived. You wrenched yourself out of my swollen belly in dirt and blood. And you were little and ugly and wizened, and I prayed to God that you would die, too. But you lived and grew and looked like me before he took me. And he played with *you* and loved *you* and I was forgotten."

Sarah found she could not move, she was so caught up in the spell of Agatha's words. Agatha moved closer to her, and Sarah could see the orange center of her eyes.

"And then the revelation came to me. One night, with the new little baby dead at my side, I knew. I had heard of the Shakers. They had come through our town selling goods. And I knew because I was Agatha Lanyard again. The same initials. A. L. I was to be Ann Lee reborn. I should have been Mother to you all, all of you." She gestured wildly around the room with her right arm. "These are my children, Lord. Only these."

147

"Mother," Sarah pleaded.

Agatha thrust her face close to Sarah's. "But you are *not* mine. You are *his*. I have seen your eyes when you look at the brethren. I have heard you laugh. Oh, you do not fool me, missy, with your sly ways. You are filth. *Filth*. And because of you, I am filth, too. I have washed and washed, but see . . ." She held out her roughened, reddened hands. She showed them to Sarah, then to Mother Jean, then in a parody of seduction, to Father James. Walking over to him, she said, "See how I have scrubbed? All today at the Fountain I scrubbed, but they would not get clean. Not my hands. Nor here." So saying, she hoisted her skirts up to her waist.

"No!" boomed Father James's horrified voice. "Do not show yourself to me, woman." He lifted his arm against her. "You have *known* a man. But we took you in anyway. A poor widow, but we took you in. Still, you have *known* a man. You have your ways. Do not show yourself to me." His voice rose higher and higher.

Agatha dropped her skirts and laughed bitterly. "A poor widow. You still think that! I knew the Believers never take in a runaway woman without her husband's permission. So I lied. My man was not dead, though he may surely be by now. Yet such a lie is a great evil. It sits heavy on the heart. Long have I scrubbed and scrubbed. I have tried to wash myself clean."

"You will never be clean," Father James cried. "Go away. Leave this community at once. Go. I command you. *Go*."

Agatha grabbed up Father James's hand and covered it with quick little kisses. "Father, do not send me away. I want to remain with you. In your house. Here in New Vale is my only chance to stay pure. Do not make me go."

Father James pushed her away roughly and held his hand against his stomach as if the hand were injured. He spoke to the others in a kind of desperate terror. There were no traces left of his commanding presence. "She must go. At once. We are not an asylum for the madness of the world. Send her *away*."

As if suddenly awakening from a dream, Agatha stared at him and began to moan. Sarah went over to her and held her tightly, the way she would a child. Agatha did not pull back. Sarah stroked her arm and whispered, smiling sadly, "I will care for you, Mother, wherever we go."

Before anyone else could speak, Sister Ann pushed into the middle of the group. In low, funereal accents that bore no resemblance to her normal voice, she hissed at Sarah, "Your paper sins outweigh mine, yet still you dare to smile. So you are the lying daughter of a lying mother. Blood calls to blood. And you have been revealed. You are a withered branch and we are the tree. You are a crooked bough and we are the bush. You are dead to us. Dead as your blood mother would have had you. And your life is woe."

"Woe," cried Sister Elizabeth after her.

"Woe, woe, woe," sang out Brothers Jacob and Jonas together.

"Woe," came a ragged chorus of sisters. They began to circle the two women, slowly at first, shaking their fists in Sarah's and Agatha's faces. "Woe, woe, woe."

With a mewling cry like that of a small, wounded beast, Agatha tore herself from Sarah's grasp, turned, and spit on her, then pushed through the circle and ran from the room.

The men crowded in. "Woe!" they boomed at Sarah.

It was not a chorus, but an army of shouters. Their single word bore down on her. She rushed from one side of the circle to the other, trying to break through, but they were solidly against her. She did not recognize any of them. The word disguised them, lent them strength. It was an incantation as powerful as a spell.

"Woe," they cried, and again, "Woe."

She saw Abel around the edge of the circle. He was not crying out against her but instead was calling her name. She tried to reach out for him but could not. Then he disappeared from her view. So she fell to her knees and let them dash the word against her. They could be a furious river, but she would be the unmovable rock in its midst. If she cared, she would not let them know it. If her blood mother would not have her, if Abel could not come to her, what did the sound of a single word matter?

In the end she closed her fists over her ears and heard, for the first time, the silence that she carried within. It was stronger than all their shouting. It was warmer than Mother Ann's cloak. It rose up, filled her, covered her, and overwhelmed all their noise.

❧ 23. Abel

He could not move. From the moment Sarah began to speak, he had been unable to move. He watched as if paralyzed. As if he had had a shock and lost the use of his limbs.

But Sarah moved. As she talked, moved, everything she did was touched with fire and beauty and grace. Abel knew that looking at her and listening was enough for him. If she decided to tell the entire story of their midnight meeting, or denounce him, even then he would not move. Or love her less. For he did love her. Would always love her. Whether she loved him in return or not.

And then when Agatha began to speak and he saw in her movements the same grace and beauty twisted, he still could not move. But he knew that whether Sarah's Worldly mother was mad or not, whether her Worldly father lived or not, he loved Sarah. For it was neither mother nor father, but daughter that he loved. And she was good and honest and loyal and true, no matter what any of the others said.

He would do anything for her, though she asked for nothing. And when the sisters and then the brothers began to shout against her, spurred on by the warring gift, he found he could move again. And he rushed to save her. But he was too late to help. He threw himself again and again against the outer perimeter of their circle but could not break through to her. He could not break through the whirling lines of chanters no matter how he tried.

All he could think of then was to find Sister Agatha. Find Sarah's mother. Find Sister Agatha, who had bolted from the room, out through the double doors that led to the outside. He would bring her back and so calm them all. He turned away from the screaming circle and dashed out the open doors.

It took him long moments to find his way in the dark. At first he could see nothing plainly, only large hulking shadows. But when his eyes adjusted to the dark, he saw that Sister Agatha was not near the Dwelling House.

He ran along the paths. He tried the doors of the Herb House, the Dyeing and Weaving Shop, the Brethren's Shop. Only the Wash House was open, but after a quick search he knew it was empty. That left only the barn.

His footsteps crunched loudly on the driveway as he ran toward the barn. He could still hear the shouting of "Woe, woe," coming through the open doors of the Dwelling House behind him. It made him move faster. The big barn door squeaked as he jerked it open.

"Agatha," he cried out. "Sister Agatha, are you here?" He did not know if his voice would frighten her even more, but he had to try.

He heard the cows and oxen lowing and grunting their agitation downstairs. He wondered if Sister Agatha, blundering in the darkened barn, might have set them off. He found the stairs. Stumbling down them, he bumped his head on the low lintel.

He called out again. "Sister, please, please come back. Come back to Meeting."

A sudden movement by his face startled him. He put his hands up over his head. It was only a dove flying across the vast dark barn.

Pushing his way past several cows, he patted them gently on their soft flanks to quiet them. In the dark he could not distinguish them, and so he used their names indiscriminately. "There, Apostle. Ho, Jerusalem. Hush, Leviticus." Their skin rolled in fear under his fingers like the ripples of a pond.

It was then that he heard the sound, a kind of slow, cadenced, quiet creaking above the cows' heads. Perhaps that was what was disturbing them. He put his hands up and walked between two of the cows toward the center mow where they fed. His fingers touched something that slipped away from his grasp. He found it again. It was cloth. Before he knew what it was for sure, he was crying out, "Oh, God, no," as if his mouth had already accepted what his mind and heart would not.

He felt her skirts, her dangling legs. She twisted away from his grasp, then spun slowly, around and around and around.

There was no way he could get her down from the first floor. He would have to retrace his steps, coming at her from above.

Gasping for breath, he pushed past the cows.

He went around the stanchions, up the stairs. He bumped against a wagon, then felt cautiously until he came to the railing. Leaning over, he found the place where she was hanging. She had used her neckerchief. One end was tied to the railing. He could feel the top of her cap as she spun away from his touch.

He stood up, his mind a morass. Finally he thought of the tool room. He blundered into it, grabbed up an ax from the wall. Dashing back to the railing, he cut through the kerchief with two swift chops. He heard the body fall heavily into the hay below.

He left the ax and ran back downstairs, past the agitated cows mooing their indignation. When he found her body and picked it up tenderly in his arms, he was surprised at how light she was, and how warm.

Somehow he got out of the barn. He went down the driveway path, through the white gate, past the bushes where he had waited that night. The shadows he cast seemed blacker than the sky.

The Dwelling House was silent now. The warring gift had ceased. He felt it must have ended the moment Agatha had ended her life.

Though he had only once before been part of a warring gift, when Brother Jackson has miscounted money and lost a good part of a month's profits for the community, Abel remembered how it had ended. With the sobbing confession of the miscreant and the fevered reconciliations of them all. He thought suddenly of Sarah's weeping in the barn and cursed himself for leaving her to weep here, alone. He could hate his beloved brothers and sisters if they forced her to break down. Then he looked again at Agatha's body in his arms — a *woman's* body in his arms — and wondered if he had made the right choice.

Marching through the open doors, Abel was not surprised to find the brothers and sisters sitting quietly on the benches in their proper places. Hands folded, they were praying. Or else they were waiting. He would never be sure which. He looked around and found Mother Jean. Carrying his pathetic burden over to her, he placed the body gently on the floor by her feet.

"I . . . I did not find her soon enough," he said, and then could not say another word. But he did not have to. Sister Agatha's broken neck, her swollen tongue, were all the explanation necessary.

Mother Jean shook her head slowly. Then at last she knelt down and, untying her own neckerchief, placed it over Sister Agatha's face. When she stood up again she went over to where Sarah was still kneeling. She held out her hand. When Sarah did not move, she said, "Come, my child. Come and mourn your sister. She was a poor, misgoverned soul, but she did the only thing she could think of to set both of you free."

Sarah stood then. She looked at Mother Jean and said in a soft voice, " 'Tis a gift to be free." She did not seem to expect any response.

They went over and stood together, Mother Jean with her arm around Sarah's shoulders, Sarah with her arm around Mother Jean's waist.

Father James cleared his throat twice. Then he

155

began to preach in that special nasal voice he used in Meeting. "And I say unto you that to take a life, whether it is your own or another's, is an anathema to God. The Fires of Hell are ready for such a one. She will not return to Paradise. She is never to be mentioned in this family again."

Mother Jean turned on him with a quiet fury. *"Bury* the dead, James. Do not deny them. *Bury* the dead. Let me exhume the living." Her arm still around Sarah's shoulder, she led her from the room.

Father James was so startled that his mouth did not close for a long time after the others had filed out past him. Only Sister Tabitha, Brother Abel, and Brother Eben stayed with him to watch over the body until Mother Jean's expected return.

✿ 24. Sarah

U pstairs in her room, Sarah sank back against Mother Jean and let her head be soothed. Mother Jean smelled of fresh soap and a sweet-sour perspiration. Sarah felt she would know that smell anywhere.

"How do you feel, child?" asked Mother Jean.

"I do not feel anything, Mother," Sarah answered. "And that frightens me. I feel nothing except a numbness. Yet I loved Agatha. She was my sister

156

and my mother, and I *should* feel a great sorrow. But I only feel numb."

"It will pass. Like pride and vanity and life itself. It will pass. That is one of God's greatest gifts to us: that things pass."

"How do you know?" Sarah asked. "How can you be so sure?"

"I know because I, too, have had to mourn and let go."

"You?"

Mother Jean nodded. Sarah could feel her body move with the motion.

"I was married in the World. And I had a child. A little girl. And her name, like yours, was Sara. And when my husband and child died from influenza, I was filled with that same terrible numbness, as if I had died myself. Friends, desperate to cheer me, brought me to a Sabbath Meeting at Hancock Village. They thought watching those funny Shakers go through their funny paces would make me laugh. They only wanted to pull me back from the edge of numbness and of death. But without meaning to, they thrust me into life. Life eternal. I was twenty-two then. I am fifty-two now. Thirty years I have had of Paradise, dear child. The numbness passes."

"But you chose to come here, Mother. You chose. I was given no choice." It was out. At last. The dreadful words. Sarah was not even horrified at having said them.

"You did no choosing, true," said Mother Jean, "because you were chosen. That should be enough. Now, get into your nightclothes. Then go to sleep. You will see, the numbness passes."

She left the room and signaled the girls to enter. They came in and undressed quickly, climbing into their beds without their usual quiet chatter.

Sister Ann looked over at Sarah. "You must feel cleansed now. The warring gift scours clean. Do you not feel better?"

"No," said Sarah. "But I am sure, Sister Ann, that you do."

Sarah's sarcasm was lost on Ann. "Oh, I do, I do," she answered. "It was glorious." She leaned out of bed and picked up the round box from her candlestand. Opening it, she showed it to the others. "See, it is empty. I have burned all my dreams."

"Oh, Sister Ann, then *you* are clean, too," cried Elizabeth. She threw her covers off and ran to Ann's bed. Hugging the glowing Ann, Elizabeth said, "Now we can be loving sisters again."

Mary, still lying in her bed, sang up to the ceiling, "Clean, clean, clean."

Sarah sat up wearily. She looked over at Sister Ann. "Is that your choice?"

The three girls looked back uneasily.

"Is there any other?" Ann asked.

Sarah stood up. "There are always choices," she said. "Yes, even if there are not, I *choose* to believe it is so." She plucked her cloak from the peg and slung it around her shoulders. Then she started out the door.

"But where are you going, Sister?" Elizabeth asked, her voice for the first time filled with a dreadful uncertainty.

"To make *my* choice," said Sarah. Then she was gone.

She went down the stairs intending to find Mother Jean. She could always talk to Mother Jean. She would explain the words in the note and tell her of the midnight meeting with Abel. She would talk of how she felt. Mother Jean would know what to do.

She expected only Mother Jean to be in the Dining Hall. At the worst, she thought, Sister Tabit would be there as well. But when she came into the room, there were five of them standing there, and the linen-draped body was no longer in sight. Mother Jean, Sister Tabit, and Brother Eben stood close together. Father James was standing apart from them near the door. They were listening intently to Brother Abel. He was speaking about his search for Agatha, his hands telling part of his tale.

They all heard her enter at the same time and stared. She knew she was immodestly dressed and, blushing, drew the cloak closed with one hand. There was nothing she could do about her capless head, with her hair standing wildly around her shoulders. She did not care.

As she came into the room, the numbness began to trickle out of her like the sand in a sand clock. And although she did not know what might replace that feeling, she knew that, with Abel's help, it would be something solid and real. In that moment she made her real choice. Holding out her hands, she met Abel halfway across the room.

"Is *this*, then, the result of our talk, Brother Abel?" asked Father James in disgust. "And the culmination of our years of selfless care? The raising up of a poor orphan has given rise to this, this greasy union, this fleshy, soft love? But I am not surprised. No, no, I had already suspected that you would be Brother *Un*able. Your old name, I recall. Prophetic, was it not? Brother Unable. Unable to live the *un*sullied life."

"No more, James. No more," cautioned Mother Jean, raising her hand. "Even the angel who expelled Adam and Eve from the first garden had the good grace not to gloat. They have already been through much tonight, these young ones. Is it not enough that now they must leave Eden tomorrow and never return?"

"Never return?" The words assaulted Sarah suddenly, harder than any blow dealth by Agatha's wooden spoon. She had not really thought beyond that night's choosing. She had not really considered giving something up in order to get. To *never* return. But as she had not broken down in the warring meeting, so now she would not let her face mirror her fear. She set her teeth together. But she felt her hand tremble in Abel's.

"Greasy union," Father James repeated. "And I will not have it demonstrated so boldly within the sanctity of this holy house. The sooner the two of you leave, the sooner we can cleanse ourselves of this abomination. You must leave tomorrow." He glared at them, them turned and walked out of the hall. Over his shoulder he cried out his parting gift. "May you have no good of your self-contamination."

Brother Eben, leaning heavily on his cane, walked to the doors. Almost apologetically he closed them on Father James's retreating figure. Then he seemed to breathe a sigh of relief as he snicked the latches

160

into place. He remained standing by the door, though whether guarding those inside the Dining Hall with him or the other Believers outside was not clear.

Sister Tabit went to one of the benches lining the walls and sat down slowly. She patted her upper lip and waited.

At last Mother Jean spoke, her head nodding up and down in that familiar, comforting way. "Ah, Sara, why did you not confide in me before this? I could have saved you all this pain, my child. *All* this pain. But now that you two have demonstrated your Worldly love in such a public way — and before Father James, most of all — there is no saving you. You cannot stay. You must leave and go out into the World. I wish, oh, my dear Sara, how I wish it were not so." She dabbed for a moment at her eyes, then drew herself up and spoke with less emotion. "Adam and Eve made a place for themselves in the World, too. It was not an easy place. It was not a simple place. It was not a Shaker place. But it was a place for themselves, nonetheless.

"Perhaps, my dear son of Adam, my dear daughter of Eve, that place is where your true gifts lie, for I see now that they are not to be found here." When she finished speaking, there was no color left in her cheeks, and she seemed, to Sarah, to have suddenly grown old.

"Oh, Mother," Sarah cried, pulling her hand from Abel's grip. She ran over and knelt before Mother Jean. "Tell me I have made the right choice. *Promise* me I will find my gifts out there." She

161

put her arms around Mother Jean's skirts and held on tightly.

Mother Jean did not touch her. "I cannot tell you what is right any more, child. You are beyond my counseling. But this much I think I have learned. Sometimes a mother helps most by not helping too much. Sometimes she can best give by giving away."

"That is a riddle," Sarah complained.

"No less true for that," said Mother Jean. "In time the meaning may come to you." She bent over and lifted Sarah to her feet.

"When I am a mother, too?" asked Sarah, beginning to understand.

"Perhaps. We must each make our own meaning."

"We will make *ours* together, Sarah." It was Abel, finding his voice at last. He held out his hand, and Sarah turned back to him. "If love gives meaning to life, you will have all the love I can give."

Standing before him, she looked up into his face. She saw neither great sorrow nor great joy there, but what she did see strengthened her.

"Yes," Sarah said. "I believe you will." Putting her hand in his, she turned to Mother Jean. "I will not ask your blessing, Mother, for I know you cannot give it to me now."

"I can and I will, child," said Mother Jean. "To be a Shaker is not to be entirely without personal choice."

Sarah bit her lip. "But . . . Father James will . . ." Sarah could not go on.

Brother Eben smiled somberly, and Sister Tabit lifted her head higher as they waited for Mother Jean's answer.

"What can Father James do to me?" asked Mother Jean, smiling wanly. "We both, together, head this family, neither higher than the other. But I will tell you this about us. Father James is too good and too pure. He knows himself innocent, and so he demands only justice. I, on the other hand, am a weaker vessel and know myself guilty of many things. Therefore I understand the quality of mercy."

Sarah looked at Mother Jean. "I do not want your mercy."

Mother Jean folded her hands in front of her again, right thumb over left, to stop the hands from shaking. "You have it nonetheless. And my blessing as well. Now go to bed, girl. Tomorrow, as Father James wills it, you and Brother Abel must leave. I cannot go against his wishes on this. There is no longer a place in Eden for you. *And* there will be much for all of us to do. There are three of my children that I must bury. You and Abel — and poor Sister Agatha."

Sarah suddenly began to cry, not soft whimperings, but great horrible sobs that seemed torn out of her. Mother Jean held her, saying nothing, till at last she stopped. Only her shoulders kept shaking as if she could control everything but them.

Brother Eben opened the doors.

Sarah pulled away from the security of Mother Jean's arms and went out the open doors. Behind her came Abel. They walked to opposite ends of the Dwelling House.

When Sarah looked back, the doors were closed. A stranger stood at the hall's end.

Tomorrow, she thought, looking at him and conscious suddenly of the pain in her throat from crying and not crying. Tomorrow he will be all of my life. And I will be all of his.

She lifted her hand, but whether as a benediction or a farewell she was not sure. Then she climbed the stairs to the second floor.

Abel was there at the end of the hall, a dark shadow on the shadow side of the house. This time it was he who lifted a hand.

Then they went into their separate sleeping rooms, to lie straight and sleepless until dawn.

May 9, 1854

❧ 25. Abel

A bel was up at first light, well before the bell. He dressed as quickly and quietly as possible and went down the stairs. He was not really surprised, though, to find Mother Jean and Sarah waiting for him.

"You must have something substantial to eat first," said Mother Jean. "It is already on the table. There will also be a sack of flour, a hundred dollars, your own clothes, and a mule. You will have to choose the one you want from the barn. I trust you, of course, to choose fairly."

"I understand," Abel said.

"But," Sarah put in, "what of bed linens? What of foodstuffs and . . ."

"Nothing more," said Mother Jean. "And yet you will find that we are being more than generous."

"And if I write to you, Mother," asked Sarah, "will you answer?"

"No."

"If I come for a visit?"

"You will be turned back at the gate."

Sarah hung her head.

"So eat quickly, Sara Barker and Abel Church, and be gone. Before Father James and the others come down." She turned from them, but Abel heard her whisper to herself, "and before my heart breaks more." Then she left to sound the morning bell.

Abel went out to the barn to pick the mule while Sarah went upstairs to pack her few things. In the daylight the barn was as sturdy and well-made as ever, but Abel fancied he could distinguish dry rot in the beams. He avoided the place where Agatha had fallen.

Looking over the five mules, he found one that seemed just right, a placid gray named Anthem. The bridle he chose was old but still serviceable. As he led Anthem down the driveway, Brother Joshua limped up and took the reins from his hand.

"How did you know?" Abel began.

"In many ways," Joshua mused. "New Vale is a small town. News travels. Especially bad news. You were not at the table, nor was a certain sister whose name is Woe. I can calculate, boy."

"Her name is not Woe. It is Sarah," said Abel snappishly. "With an *h*."

"Springtime Sarah."

"This one is not like yours," Abel answered. "I love her. She is forever."

"She had better be," Joshua said. "If I have to

lose you, it had better be to someone you love, someone who is forever. Not all people out in the World are fools full of the jimjams. And I will always expect more from you — and from your Sarah."

Abel suddenly rushed over to the old man and embraced him. Then slowly he said, "Been thinking, Brother Joshua."

Joshua's answer, though predictable, was slow in coming. "Not always a good thing, thinking," he said finally.

"I have been thinking for some time that you should come with us. Come with Sarah and me. Into the World. We will take care of you."

Joshua stood for a moment more before moving out of the circle of Abel's arms. He wiped his face with a white square of linen and blew his nose loudly. "It would never work, boy. Each time I go out into the World selling, I have considered it. But it would not work. Look around you. *This* is my world now. My world and my choice. Oh, I do not fancy everything here. All that dancing and that foo-farrah can get a mite tiresome to a lame old man like me. But I can do here what I do best, and that is farming. Without worrying myself about the bank or what the neighbors think. I put in seed and reap a harvest and have folk who know how to leave me alone and who know how to count on me. There is no way I am going to leave New Vale except in my coffin. Still, it will be a mighty poorer place without you in it. I mean to say I am going to miss you, boy."

"I will miss you, too, Joshua. You have been . . . you have been my closest friend."

"I have been more than that. I have been your

167

father, more than that self-righteous prig ever has been. And you are not to forget that."

Abel smiled. "No, no, I will not forget." He held out his hand. "Good-bye. Father."

Joshua shook his head. "Not yet. Not yet. I want to walk the two of you to the gate. I have already told Elder Eben I plan to do it instead of going over to the burying ground. Too many going under and too few coming in the door."

They walked past the Dwelling House to the gate. Sarah was waiting. The sack of flour was by her side. She held a white pillow sack containing her clothes and brush and a single round box.

"Mother Jean slipped the box into the sack at the last minute. She said it contains two papers. One is the note I wrote for you. Mother had not read it. She said, 'That is your dream, Sara, not mine. Keep it safe.' The other paper has my father's name on it: Abraham Barker. And a place. Northwick, Massachusetts. It was in with Sister Agatha's things. Mother Jean found it there. If he is still alive, someone in Northwick may know." She held out her hand to Abel and put a small envelope in it. "The money is here."

Abel stopped her. "You keep the money safe, Sarah. I have to get my own clothes. This is our mule. His name is Anthem."

"Anthem," said Sarah. "I like that. It has a good beginning sound."

Joshua cleared his throat.

Blushing, Abel said, "Brother Joshua is seeing us off."

"Thank you, Brother," said Sarah, looking down at the ground. She found it hard to look at him.

168

"Look up, girl. Look me in the eye. That is how it is done in the World," said Joshua.

Sarah looked up slowly.

"There, that was not so hard."

"Yes. Yes, it was," Sarah said.

Joshua began to muse aloud. "Northwick, Massachusetts. Northwick, you say. I believe we sometimes pass close by that town when we go selling. I expect sometimes we could pass right through."

"Could you?" Sarah asked breathlessly. "I mean, if we were there and it was not far and Father James would . . ."

"Father James. Yes," Joshua's face grew thoughtful. "I expect we could. In fact, I know we could. Sometimes."

Sarah smiled.

Abel left and ran back to the Dwelling House. He took the stairs two at a time and clattered into his room. He snatched his Sunday clothes from the hook and his shoes from the floor, then sped back down the stairs. He was gone only a few minutes. Sarah and Joshua were still smiling at one another, but they were not talking.

"Here," Abel said breathlessly, "put these in the sack with your clothes."

"Your clothes. Touching mine?" For a moment Sarah was shocked. Then she laughed. "Where else?"

"You can ride Anthem and I will walk beside you."

"No," said Sarah, "Anthem can carry our things, but you and I will walk out together."

Abel tied the mouths of the sacks and slung them over the placid mule's back. Joshua opened the gate and watched as they walked side by side down the

169

road, not quite touching. The mule ambled along beside them.

They were still within hearing distance when Brother John came running to Joshua at the gate.

"It is Apostle," he was calling as he ran. "Apostle. She is going to have her calf. Brother Andrew says to hurry."

Abel heard and looked over his shoulder. He watched as Joshua turned toward the excited boy. Abel waved once, then twice as Joshua closed the gate and limped away with Brother John.

Sarah did not look back.

❧ 26. Meeting

It had been a horrible Sabbath, a simply horrible day, Mother Jean thought as she marched down the stairs. She tried not to think of the burying ground where they had sung Sister Agatha into her cold grave. Soon that mound of earth would be as orderly as the rest and they could set the headstone on it. It would be another sturdy stone in a forest of stones, bearing only Agatha's name and dates. More upright, Mother Jean thought uncharitably, than Sister Agatha had been in life. The image of the neat rows of stones would not leave her, and she wondered suddenly what kind of graveyard awaited Sara and Abel in their time. She shook her head, "I *must* be getting old," she mumbled to herself.

Beside her marched Eldress Tabit, the events of the day already carefully erased from her mind as she concentrated on the coming Sabbath Meeting. And on the fact that her shoes were too tight for comfort. Pleasure and pain were always twinned in Eldress Tabit's mind.

Sisters Martha and Faith walked next, their shoulders touching every second step. They looked grim and, in fact, had looked that way since the word about Sara's departure had made the rounds of the Believers. Faith had spent the afternoon in the Nurse Shop with a sick headache, and Martha had spoiled a batch of madder dye — something she had not done in years.

The sisters who marched behind them were as silent as usual. Only the last three, little more than girls, showed signs of the taxing nature of the day. Sister Mary had been weeping on and off during the morning. Sister Ann had refused to believe what had happened and instead kept looking everywhere for Sara. "My best friend," she had called Sara several times since Elizabeth's surprise confession to her that Elizabeth had been the tattler. Sister Elizabeth had simply not spoken to anyone all afternoon. As the three came down the stairs, tears started again in Mary's eyes, and Ann's shredded handkerchief, which she kept balled up between her clasped hands, fell to the floor. Elizabeth, marching last in line alone, trod on it and never noticed.

On the men's stair Father James led them down. His step was almost jaunty. He felt purged, felt that

171

the entire community had been purged. The three deaths — for he thought of every defection as a death — had been positive steps. Now the Believers could return to their unsullied lives. If he had known how to whistle, he might have been tempted.

Next to Father James, his mouth sour and his thoughts dark, marched Brother Eben. He was many years older than Father James, and this was not the first time he had seen a young couple thrust from the community. He doubted it would be the last. He wondered, as he always did, about the wisdom of such a precipitate, forced exile. Given more time, he mused, most young Shakers would change their minds. He had. Years before he had thought himself ready to leave with a girl. They had even managed to meet in secret over a period of weeks. But he had said nothing to anyone else, nor had she. And the mood — for that was all it was — had passed. They had remained together in New Vale as brother and sister. His love for her now was as pure as his love for any of the others. He did not even dream of Sister Faith anymore. It was much better so.

Brother Frank and Brother Joshua walked close behind. Frank patted his vest pocket to be sure he had placed his pipe there. He had not really gotten over the surprise of Abel's leaving. Such a shock, really; such a good worker gone.

Joshua thought of his last glimpse of the two of them. He had suddenly realized how young they were, the boy and girl. Young and without protection. Perhaps he *should* have gone out with them. But he dismissed that thought quickly. He was not really needed out there. His place was here. It was best that

172

he leave them to cope with their own coming trials. It would bring them closer together, bind them in a way that marriage vows alone could never do.

The rest of the men marching down the stairs were as orderly as usual. The last four — Andrew and Jonas, Jacob, and John — wore strange expressions. But while Jonas's face still bore traces of jealous resentment, and Andrew's was creased with a kind of uncertain compassion, only John's was truly bereft. He had been told that Abel was dead and so thought that what he had seen had been a ghost on the road going out of New Vale. For the rest of his life he would rush to the gate whenever anyone in the community died, expecting to see a ghost. The comings and goings of others on the road puzzled him completely. He would never get it straight.

The two columns of marchers walked out of the doors and crossed the dirt road. The full moon lit the sky. An owl heralded their approach from a pine tree overlooking the Meeting House. As they came closer, the owl took off on silent wings up Holy Hill, its eyes alert for prey. It stopped once on an oak that had been badly split by the harsh winter, calling out again. The sound of its voice floated down to the marchers.

Ranged down the road was a procession of small surreys and coaches, the horses standing quietly in their traces. As usual, many of the World's folks had come to the Sabbath Meeting to watch the Believers of New Vale pray. They would be inside already, sitting quietly on the benches arranged around the edges of the room. Brother John nudged Andrew's side and pointed to one splendid pair of matched bays near the south end of the building. Andrew casually slapped John's hand down as they followed the rest inside.

Hanging coats and cloaks on the wall pegs, the brethren and sisters came in their separate doors. Then they found their places by the small dark pegs set flush into the light-colored wide-board floors. They straightened their shoulders. The men sucked in their stomachs and threw out their chests. The sisters gave a last-minute tug to their skirts.

Sabbath Meeting had begun.

Brother Eben stepped back into the doorway. Leaning on his cane, he drew the tonometer from his pocket and struck the string. The A could be heard by all. The song they started had no words, just "la-la-la's," and at the second measure, in perfect time, the Believers began to dance. It was a slow, controlled, ordered shuffle. Only Brother Eben stood aside.

In two lines the men and women moved three steps forward. Then, with a quick tip-tap of their toes, they marched three steps back. The brothers set off to the left, the sisters going right. Singing still, they continued dancing in time. It was a slow, measured step that reminded them all of the deaths of the day.

But soon they had spun around and, at Mother Jean's urging, begun a different dance. She gave them several tuneful measures with her lovely voice, and they spun into "Mother's Square," a fast-paced, lively frolic.

As suddenly, that dance ended and they slipped into a complicated pattern of concentric circles. Round and round they went, spinning and dipping,

174

gliding and high-stepping. To the onlookers it was as well choreographed as a theater show. Only the dancers knew that there was meaning to the steps. The marching was the soul's trip toward heaven, the circles stood for the cycles of belief.

It went on for almost an hour till the intermission, when they sat silently on the benches reserved for them. The sisters spread white handkerchiefs on their laps so that the perspiration from their damp palms would not stain the purity of their dresses. They were up again in minutes for another hour of dance and song. The last dance, sung with words, was another slow, solemn shuffle recalling the morning's grim tasks and the hope for a better day to come.

"I understand they practice all the time," a young girl watching from the sidelines said quietly to her mother. "Cousin Leilah drove down the road once with her beau and said she saw them marching up and down the road, singing."

Her father overheard. "Your cousin Leilah has a tongue that will get her into trouble. And they must spend *some* time farming. I have never seen anything like those fields and orchards."

Next to him a young man whispered into his fiancée's ear, "They certainly do dance up a sweat. I guess there is something to be said for the passionless life."

She looked at him coyly from under lowered lids. "And what is that, pray?"

He chuckled and put his hand over hers. "When you look at me like that, I just plain forget."

She giggled.

* * *

Father James's face glowed with perspiration, but he refused to acknowledge it by wiping it away. There was a stitch in his side, and he was glad of it. He looked over at Mother Jean and smiled. She looked back, nodding slowly. Then she gave a quick, faint smile before marching out the door, trailing the line of sisters behind her.

Sabbath Meeting was over. After a good night's sleep, another week at New Vale would begin. Mother Jean had a quick, sharp picture of Sister Sara's beautiful young face looking up at her, begging to know if she had made the right choice.

"Right choice? Of course. She made the *only* choice. In Paradise," Mother Jean reminded herself sternly, "there is room only for the angels."

❧ 27. Epilogue

For over fifty years more the Believers at New Vale continued to work together. A small typhoid epidemic, brought in by one of the World's folk hired to help with an overabundant harvest, swept through the Believers' ranks in 1862. Father James, Brother Eben, and Brother John died within days of one another, along with thirteen other brothers and sisters. Father Jackson became a well-liked but ineffectual leader for some twenty years, and at his death, Father Andrew ruled the male line. First Brother Frank, then Brother Jacob became Elder.

It was Sister Elizabeth who took over after Mother Jean died in her eighty-seventh year. Black Mary had been Eldress for some time then, and neither of them ever spoke of the long-departed Sister Sara or of Sister Ann, who had run off on her fortieth birthday with a storekeeper from the neighboring town.

Brother Joshua made many selling trips through Northwick until younger brothers took over that labor. Confined to New Vale, he went strange at the century's turning and spoke only to the animals thereafter. He even called them by human names.

In 1910, with only seventeen Believers left in the Church family, and no children in the children's order or any newcomers in the gathering order, New Vale closed its doors. The remaining Shakers moved to Sabbathday Lake in Maine, after leasing their fields and orchards to farmers in the valley.

As for Sarah and Abel, it took them four months of walking and hiring-out along the way to find Northwick. Abraham Barker was not only still alive, he was overwhelmed at the reunion. He had never thought to see his only child again. When his wife had run off without warning, without even leaving a note, he had become a recluse. At forty-seven, he was already an old man. But the arrival of Sarah and Abel added years to his life.

Abel and Sarah were married within days of finding Northwick, *after* Sarah had gotten her father's neglected house in order. She refused, she said, to be married in a house where so much dust and disorder reigned.

Abel rebuilt the smithy and then apprenticed for less than a year with old Abraham, learning blacksmithing with an ease that delighted them both. Except for a year in the Union army, where he was invalided out with a leg wound suffered while rescuing a drummer boy, Abel worked at the smithy. In his capable hands the shop thrived, and his dedication and honesty won him many admirers in the town. He was twice elected mayor.

Sarah taught school before the birth of their first child and gave singing lessons thereafter. The Congregational minister wanted her to lead the church choir, but she allowed that she had had enough of houses of God and preferred to worship in God's own house, by which she meant the top of a wooded hillside behind the smithy that was covered with wild blueberries in the summer. Though it shocked the minister at first, he soon became her lifelong friend, and, besides, all her children grew up to pray in his church.

Abraham Barker was the best of grandfathers. His greatest delight was to dandle his grandchildren on his knees. He knew a wealth of singing games, and when he died at sixty-seven, he was much mourned by his family.

When Sarah departed life in her ninety-first year, her five children and nineteen grandchildren had the following gravestone carved. Under the picture of a smiling angel's face were the words:

SARAH BARKER CHURCH
Loving daughter, beloved wife and mother
1840–1931
Her gifts were laughter, loyalty, and love.

Within a year the stone had tilted, touching the one next to it in the churchyard. That other stone read:

ABEL CHURCH
1838–1900
His honesty made his living,
His family made his life.

No one in the town of Northwick would have ever dared push the two stones apart.

About the Author

Jane Yolen is an experienced editor, teacher, and the author of more than sixty outstanding children's books. *The Gift of Sarah Barker* is her first young adult novel. Born in New York City, she is a graduate of Smith College. She lives with her husband and their three children on a farm in Massachusetts.